THE HEMINGWAY HOAX

"Just speakin', you know, in theory. Like some guy who really knows Hemingway, suppose he makes up some stories that're like those old ones, finds some seventy-five-year-old paper and an old, what do you call them, not a word processor—"

"Typewriter."

"Whatever. Think he could pass 'em off for the real thing?"

"Sure he could. Be a fortune in it."

"How much? A million bucks?"

"A million . . . maybe. Well, sure. The last new Hemingway made at least that much, allowing for inflation. And he's more popular now."

Castle took a big gulp of beer and set his glass down decisively. "So what the hell are we waiting for?"

Baird's bland smile faded. "You're serious?"

**Also by the same author,
and available from NEL:**

The Long Habit of Living

About the author

Joe Haldeman was born in Oklahoma City in 1943. He qualified for his BSc in astronomy and for his MFA in English. Since winning the Hugo and Nebula Awards for his novel *The Forever War*, he has been an active and influential force in the science fiction community.

He and his wife Gay have been married for the last twenty-five years. They divide their time between Cambridge, Massachusetts, where he currently teaches creative writing at MIT, and Gainesville, Florida.

The Hemingway Hoax

Joe Haldeman

NEW ENGLISH LIBRARY
Hodder and Stoughton

British Library C.I.P.

Haldeman, Joe, *1943–*
The Hemingway hoax.
I. Title
813.54[F]

ISBN 0-450-55195-4

Printed and bound in Great Britain for Hodder and Stoughton Paperbacks, a division of Hodder and Stoughton Ltd., Mill Road, Dunton Green, Sevenoaks, Kent TN13 2YA (Editorial Office: 47 Bedford Square, London WC1B 3DP) by Clays Ltd., St Ives plc.

He had already learned that there was only one day at a time and that it was always the day you were in. It would be today until it was tonight and tomorrow it would be today again. This was the main thing he had learned so far.

—from "The Last Good Country"

THE HEMINGWAY HOAX

1 The Torrents of Spring

Our story begins in a run-down bar in Key West, not so many years from now. The bar is not the one Hemingway drank at, nor yet the one that claims to be the one he drank at, because they are both too expensive and full of tourists. This bar, in a more interesting part of town, is a Cuban place. It is neither clean nor well-lighted, but has cold beer and good strong Cuban coffee. Its cheap prices and rascally charm are what bring together the scholar and the rogue.

Their first meeting would be of little significance to either at the time, though the scholar, John Baird, would never forget it. John Baird was not capable of forgetting anything.

Key West is lousy with writers, mostly poor writers, in one sense of that word or the other. Poor people did not interest our rogue, Sylvester Castlemaine, so at first he didn't take any special note of the man sitting in the corner scribbling on a yellow pad. Just another would-be writer, come down to see whether some of Papa's magic would rub off. Not worth the energy of a con.

But Castle's professional powers of observation caught at a detail or two and focused his attention. The man was wearing jeans and a faded flannel shirt, but his shoes were expensive Italian loafers. His beard had been trimmed by a barber. He was drinking Heineken. The pen he was scribbling with was a fat

Mont Blanc Diplomat, two hundred bucks on the hoof, discounted. Castle got his cup of coffee and sat at a table two away from the writer.

He waited until the man paused, sat the pen down, took a drink. "Writing a story?" Castle said.

The man blinked at him. "No . . . just an article." He put the cap on the pen with a crisp snap. "An article about stories. I'm a college professor."

"Publish or perish," Castle said.

The man relaxed a bit. "Too true." He riffled through the yellow pad. "This won't help much. It's not going anywhere."

"Tell you what . . . bet you a beer it's Hemingway or Tennessee Williams."

"Too easy." He signaled the bartender. "Dos cervezas. Hemingway, the early stories. You know his work?"

"Just a little. We had to read him in school—*The Old Man and the Fish*? And then I read a couple after I got down here." He moved over to the man's table. "Name's Castle."

"John Baird." Open, honest expression; not too promising. You can't con somebody unless he thinks he's conning you. "Teach up at Boston."

"I'm mostly fishing. Shrimp nowadays." Of course Castle didn't normally fish, not for things in the sea, but the shrimp part was true. He'd been reduced to heading shrimp on the *Catalina* for five dollars a bucket. "So what about these early stories?"

The bartender set down the two beers and gave Castle a weary look.

"Well . . . they don't exist." John Baird carefully poured the beer down the side of his glass. "They were stolen. Never published."

"So what can you write about them?"

"Indeed. That's what I've been asking myself." He took a sip of the beer and settled back. "Seventy-four years ago they were stolen. December, 1922. That's really what got me working on them; thought I would do a paper, a monograph, for the seventy-fifth anniversary of the occasion."

It sounded less and less promising, but this was the first imported beer Castle had had in months. He slowly savored the bite of it.

"He and his first wife, Hadley, were living in Paris. You know about Hemingway's early life?"

"Huh-uh. Paris?"

"He grew up in Oak Park, Illinois. That was kind of a prissy, self-satisfied suburb of Chicago."

"Yeah, I been there."

"He didn't like it. In his teens, he sort of ran away from home, went down to Kansas City to work on a newspaper.

"World War One started, and like a lot of kids, Hemingway couldn't wait to get a piece of it. He couldn't join the army because of a bad eye, so he joined the Red Cross and went off to drive ambulances in Italy. Take cigarettes and chocolate to the troops.

"That almost killed him. He was just doing his cigarettes-and-chocolate routine and an artillery round came in, killed the guy next to him, tore up another, riddled Hemingway with shrapnel. He claims then that he picked up the wounded guy and carried him back to the trench, in spite of being hit in the knee by a machine-gun bullet."

"What do you mean, 'claims'?"

"You're too young to have been in Vietnam."

"Yeah."

"Good for you. I was hit in the knee by a machine-gun bullet myself, and went down on my ass and didn't get up for five weeks. He didn't carry anybody one step."

"That's interesting."

"Well, he was always rewriting his life. We all do it. But it seemed to be a compulsion with him. That's one thing that makes Hemingway scholarship challenging."

Baird poured the rest of the beer into his glass. "Anyhow, he actually was the first American wounded in Italy, and they made a big deal over him. He went back to Oak Park a war hero. He had a certain amount of success with women."

"Or so he says?"

"Right, God knows. Anyhow, he met Hadley Richardson, an older woman but quite a number, and they had a steamy courtship and got married and said the hell with it, moved to Paris to live a sort of bohemian life while Hemingway worked on perfecting his art. That part isn't bullshit. He worked diligently and he did become one of the best writers of his era. Which brings us to the lost manuscripts."

"Do tell."

"Hemingway was picking up a little extra money doing journalism. He'd gone to Switzerland to cover a peace conference for a news service. When it was over, he wired Hadley to come join him for some skiing.

"This is where it gets odd. On her own initiative, Hadley packed up all of Ernest's work. All of it. Not just the typescripts, but the handwritten first drafts and the carbons."

"That's like a Xerox?"

"Right. She packed them in an overnight bag, then packed her own suitcase. A porter at the train station, the Gare de Lyon, put them aboard for her. She left the train for a minute to find something to read—and when she came back, they were gone."

"Suitcase and all?"

"No, just the manuscripts. She and the porter searched up and down the train. But that was it. Somebody had seen the overnight bag sitting there and snatched it. Lost forever."

That did hold a glimmer of professional interest. "That's funny. You'd think they'd get a note then, like, 'If you ever want to see your stories again, bring a million bucks to the Eiffel Tower' sort of thing."

"A few years later, that might have happened. It didn't take long for Hemingway to become famous. But at the time, only a few of the literary intelligentsia knew about him."

Castle shook his head in commiseration with the long-dead thief. "Guy who stole 'em probably didn't even read English. Dumped 'em in the river."

John Baird shivered visibly. "Undoubtedly. But people have never stopped looking for them. Maybe they'll show up in some attic someday."

"Could happen." Wheels turning.

"It's happened before in literature. Some of Boswell's diaries were recovered because a scholar recognized his handwriting on an old piece of paper a merchant used to wrap a fish. Hemingway's own last book, he put together from notes that had been lost for thirty years. They were in a couple of trunks in the basement of the Ritz, in Paris." He leaned forward, excited. "Then after he died, they found another batch of papers down here, in a back room in Sloppy Joe's. It could still happen."

Castle took a deep breath. "It could be made to happen, too."

"Made to happen?"

"Just speakin', you know, in theory. Like some guy who really knows Hemingway, suppose he makes up some stories that're like those old ones, finds some seventy-five-year-old paper and an old, what do you call them, not a word processor—"

"Typewriter."

"Whatever. Think he could pass 'em off for the real thing?"

"I don't know if he could fool me," Baird said, and tapped the side of his head. "I have a freak memory: eidetic, photographic. I have just about every word Hemingway ever wrote committed to memory." He looked slightly embarrassed. "Of course that doesn't make me an expert in the sense of being able to spot a phony. I just wouldn't have to refer to any texts."

"So take yourself, you know, or somebody else who spent all his life studyin' Hemingway. He puts all he's got into writin' these stories—he knows the people who are gonna be readin' 'em; knows what they're gonna look for. And he hires like an expert forger to make the pages look like they came out of Hemingway's machine. So could it work?"

Baird pursed his lips and for a moment looked professorial. Then he sort of laughed, one syllable through his nose. "Maybe it could. A man did a similar thing when I was a boy, counterfeiting the memoirs of Howard Hughes. He made millions."

"Millions?"

"Back when that was real money. Went to jail when they found out, of course."

"And the money was still there when he got out."

"Never read anything about it. I guess so."

"So the next question is, how much stuff are we talkin' about? How much was in that old overnight bag?"

"That depends on who you believe. There was half a novel and some poetry. The short stories, there might have been as few as eleven or as many as thirty."

"That'd take a long time to write."

"It would take forever. You couldn't just 'do' Hemingway; you'd have to figure out what the stories were about, then reconstruct his early style—do you know how many Hemingway scholars there are in the world?"

"Huh-uh. Quite a few."

"Thousands. Maybe ten thousand academics who know enough to spot a careless fake."

Castle nodded, cogitating. "You'd have to be real careful. But then you wouldn't have to do all the short stories and poems, would you? You could say all you found was the part of the novel. Hell, you could sell that as a book."

The odd laugh again. "Sure you could. Be a fortune in it."

"How much? A million bucks?"

"A million . . . maybe. Well, sure. The last new Hemingway made at least that much, allowing for inflation. And he's more popular now."

Castle took a big gulp of beer and set his glass down decisively. "So what the hell are we waiting for?"

Baird's bland smile faded. "You're serious?"

2   in our time

Got a ripple in the Hemingway channel.
Twenties again?
No, funny, this one's in the 1990s. See if you can track it down?
Sure. Go down to the armory first and—
Look—no bloodbaths this time. You solve one problem and start ten more.
Couldn't be helped. It's no tea party, twentieth-century America.
Just use good judgment. That Ransom guy . . .
Manson. Right. That was a mistake.

3   A Way You'll Never Be

You can't cheat an honest man, as Sylvester Castlemaine well knew, but then again, it never hurts to find out just how honest a man is. John Baird refused his scheme, with good humor at first, but when Castle persisted, his refusal took on a sarcastic edge; maybe a tinge of outrage. He backed off and changed the subject, talking for a half hour about commercial fishing around Key West, and then said he had to run. He slipped his business card into John's shirt pocket on the way out. (Sylvester Castlemaine, Consultant, it claimed.)

John left the place soon, walking slowly through the afternoon heat. He was glad he hadn't brought the bicycle; it was pleasant to walk in the shade of the big aromatic trees, a slight breeze on his face from the Gulf side.

One could do it. One could. The problem divided itself into three parts; writing the novel fragment, forging the manuscript, and devising a suitable story about how one had uncovered the manuscript.

The writing part would be the hardest. Hemingway is easy enough to parody—one fourth of the take-home final he gave in English 733 was to write a page of Hemingway pastiche, and some of his graduate students did a credible job—but parody was exactly what one would not want to do.

It had been a crucial period in Hemingway's development, those three years of apprenticeship the lost manuscripts represented. Two stories survived, and they were maddeningly dissimilar. "My Old Man," which had slipped down behind a drawer, was itself a pastiche, reading like pretty good Sherwood Anderson, but with an O. Henry twist at the end—very unlike the bleak understated quality that would distinguish the stories that were to make Hemingway's reputation. The other, "Up in Michigan," had been out in the mail at the time of the loss. It was a lot closer to Hemingway's ultimate style, a spare and, by the standards of the time, pornographic description of a woman's first sexual experience.

John riffled through the notes on the yellow pad, a talismanic gesture, since he could have remembered any page with little effort. But the sight of the words and the feel of the paper sometimes helped him think.

One would not do it, of course. Except perhaps as a mental exercise. Not to show to anybody. Certainly not to profit from.

You wouldn't want to use "My Old Man" as the model, certainly; no one would care to publish a pastiche of a pastiche

of Anderson, now undeservedly obscure. So "Up in Michigan."
And the first story he wrote after the loss, "Out of Season,"
would also be handy. That had a lot of the true Hemingway
strength.

You wouldn't want to tackle the novel fragment, of course,
not just as an exercise, over a hundred pages . . .

Without thinking about it, John dropped into a familiar
fugue state as he walked through the run-down neighborhood,
his freak memory taking over while his body ambled along on
autopilot. This is the way he usually remembered pages. He
transported himself back to the Hemingway collection at the JFK
Library in Boston, last November, snow swirling outside the big
picture windows overlooking the harbor, the room so cold he was
wearing coat and gloves and could see his breath. They didn't
normally let you wear a coat up there, afraid you might squirrel
away a page out of the manuscript collection, but they had to
make an exception because the heat pump was down.

He was flipping through the much-thumbed Xerox of Carlos
Baker's interview with Hadley, page 52: "Stolen suitcase," Baker
asked; "lost novel?"

The typescript of her reply appeared in front of him, more
clear than the cracked sidewalk his feet negotiated: "This novel
was a knock-out, about Nick, up north in Michigan—hunting,
fishing, all sorts of experiences—stuff on the order of Big Two-
Hearted River, with more action. Girl experiences well done,
too." With an enigmatic addition, evidently in Hadley's handwriting, "Girl experiences too well done."

That was interesting. John hadn't thought about that, since
he'd been concentrating on the short stories. Too well done?
There had been a lot of talk in the eighties about Hemingway's
sexual ambiguity—*gender* ambiguity, actually—could Hadley
have been upset, sixty years after the fact, remembering some
confidence that Hemingway had revealed to the world in that
novel; something girls knew that boys were not supposed to
know? Playful pillow talk that was filed away for eventual literary
exploitation?

He used his life that way. A good writer remembered everything and then forgot it when he sat down to write, and reinvented it so the writing would be more real than the memory. Experience was important, but imagination was more important.

Maybe I would be a better writer, John thought, if I could learn how to forget. For about the tenth time today, like any day, he regretted not having tried to succeed as a writer while he still had the independent income. Teaching and research had fascinated him when he was younger, a rich boy's all-consuming hobbies, but the end of this fiscal year would be the end of the monthly checks from the trust fund. So the salary from Boston University wouldn't be mad money anymore but rent and groceries in a city suddenly expensive.

Yes, the writing would be the hard part. Then forging the manuscript, that wouldn't be easy. Any scholar would have access to copies of thousands of pages that Hemingway typed before and after the loss. Could one find the typewriter Hemingway had used? Then duplicate his idiosyncratic typing style—a moment's reflection put a sample in front of him, spaces before and after periods and commas . . .

He snapped out of the reverie as his right foot hit the first step on the back staircase up to their rented flat. He automatically stepped over the fifth step, the rotted one, and was thinking about a nice tall glass of iced tea as he opened the screen door.

"Scorpions!" his wife screamed, two feet from his face.

"What?"

"We have scorpions!" Lena grabbed his arm and hauled him to the kitchen. "Look!" She pointed at the opaque plastic skylight. Three scorpions, each about six inches long, cast sharp silhouettes on the milky plastic. One was moving.

"My word."

"Your *word*!" She struck a familiar pose, hands on hips, and glared up at the creatures. "What are we going to do about it?"

"We could name them."

"John."

"I don't know." He opened the refrigerator. "Call the bug man."

"The bug man was just here yesterday. He probably flushed them out."

He poured a glass of cold tea and dumped two envelopes of artificial sweetener into it. "I'll talk to Julio about it. But you know they've been there all along. They're not bothering anybody."

"They're bothering the hell out of *me!*"

He smiled. "Okay. I'll talk to Julio." He looked into the oven. "Thought about dinner?"

"Anything you want to cook, sweetheart. I'll be damned if I'm going to stand there with three . . . poisonous . . . arthropods staring down at me."

"Poised to jump," John said, and looked up again. There were only two visible now, which made his skin crawl.

"Julio wasn't home when I first saw them. About an hour ago."

"I'll go check." John went downstairs, and Julio, the landlord, was indeed home, but was not impressed by the problem. He agreed that it was probably the bug man, and they would probably go back to where they came from in a while, and gave John a flyswatter.

John left the flyswatter with Lena, admonishing her to take no prisoners, and walked a couple of blocks to a Chinese restaurant. He brought back a few boxes of take-out, and they sat in the living room and wielded chopsticks in silence, listening for the pitter-patter of tiny feet.

"Met a real live con man today." He put the business card on the coffee table between them.

"Consultant?" she read.

"He had a loony scheme about counterfeiting the missing stories." Lena knew more about the missing stories than 98 percent of the people who Hemingwayed for a living. John liked to think out loud.

"Ah, the stories," she said, preparing herself.

"Not a bad idea, actually, if one had a larcenous nature." He concentrated for a moment on the slippery Moo Goo Gai Pan. "Be millions of bucks in it."

He was bent over the box. She stared hard at his bald spot. "What exactly did he have in mind?"

"We didn't bother to think it through in any detail, actually. You go and find . . ." He got the slightly walleyed look that she knew meant he was reading a page of a book a thousand miles away. "Yes. A 1921 Corona portable, like the one Hadley gave him before they were married. Find some old paper. Type up the stories. Take them to Sotheby's. Spend money for the rest of your life. That's all there is to it."

"You left out jail."

"A mere detail. Also the writing of the stories. That could take weeks. Maybe you could get arrested first, write the stories in jail, and then sell them when you got out."

"You're weird, John."

"Well. I didn't give him any encouragement."

"Maybe you should've. A few million would come in handy next year."

"We'll get by."

" 'We'll get by.' You keep saying that. How do you know? You've never had to 'get by.' "

"Okay, then. We won't get by." He scraped up the last of the fried rice. "We won't be able to make the rent and they'll throw us out on the street. We'll live in a cardboard box over a heating grate. You'll have to sell your body to keep me in cheap wine. But we'll be happy, dear." He looked up at her, mooning. "Poor but happy."

"Slaphappy." She looked at the card again. "How do you know he's a con man?"

"I don't know. Salesman type. Says he's in commercial fishing now, but he doesn't seem to like it much."

"He didn't say anything about any, you know, criminal stuff he'd done in the past?"

"Huh-uh. I just got the impression that he didn't waste a lot of time mulling over ethics and morals." John held up the Mont Blanc pen. "He was staring at this, before he came over and introduced himself. I think he smelled money."

Lena stuck both chopsticks into the half-finished carton of boiled rice and set it down decisively. "Let's ask him over."

"He's a sleaze, Lena. You wouldn't like him."

"I've never met a real con man. It would be fun."

He looked into the darkened kitchen. "Will you cook something?"

She followed his gaze, expecting monsters. "If you stand guard."

4   Romance is Dead (*subtitle The Hell it is*)

"**B**e a job an' a half," Castle said, mopping up residual spaghetti sauce with a piece of garlic bread. "It's not like your Howard Hughes guy, or Hitler's notebooks."

"You've been doing some research." John's voice was a little slurred. He'd bought a half-gallon of Portuguese wine, the bottle wrapped in straw like cheap Chianti, the wine not quite that good. If you could get past the first couple of glasses, it was okay. It had been okay to John for some time now.

"Yeah, down to the library. The guys who did the Hitler notebooks—hell, nobody'd ever seen a real Hitler notebook;

they just studied his handwriting in letters and such, then read up on what he did day after day. Same with the Howard Hughes, but that was even easier, because most of the time nobody knew what the hell Howard Hughes was doing anyhow. Just stayed locked up in that room."

"The Hughes forgery nearly worked, as I recall," John said. "If Hughes himself hadn't broken silence . . ."

"Ya gotta know that took balls. 'Scuse me, Lena." She waved a hand and laughed. "Try to get away with that while Hughes was still alive."

"How did the Hitler people screw up?" she asked.

"Funny thing about that one was how many people they fooled. Afterwards, everybody said it was a really lousy fake. But you can bet that before the newspapers bid millions of dollars on it, they showed it to the best Hitler-ologists they could find, and they all said it was real."

"Because they wanted it to be real," Lena said.

"Yeah. But one of the pages had some chemical in it that wouldn't be in paper before 1945. That was kinda dumb."

"People would want the Hemingway stories to be real," Lena said quietly, to John.

John's gaze stayed fixed on the center of the table, where a few strands of spaghetti lay cold and drying in a plastic bowl. "Wouldn't be honest."

"That's for sure," Castle said cheerily. "But it ain't exactly armed robbery, either."

"A gross misuse of intellectual . . . intellectual . . ."

"It's past your bedtime, John," Lena said. "We'll clean up." John nodded and pushed himself away from the table and walked heavily into the bedroom.

Lena didn't say anything until she heard the bedsprings creak. "He isn't always like this," she said quietly.

"Yeah. He don't act like no alky."

"It's been a hard year for him." She refilled her glass. "Me too. Money."

"That's bad."

"Well, we knew it was coming. He tell you about the inheritance?"

Castle leaned forward. "Huh-uh."

"He was born pretty well off. Family had textile mills up in New Hampshire. John's grandparents died in an auto accident in the forties and the family sold off the mills—good timing, too. They wouldn't be worth much today."

"Then John's father and mother died in the sixties, while he was in college. The executors set up a trust fund that looked like it would keep him in pretty good shape forever. But he wasn't interested in money. He even joined the army, to see what it was like."

"Jesus."

"Afterwards, he carried a picket sign and marched against the war—you know, Vietnam."

"Then he finished his Ph.D. and started teaching. The trust fund must have been fifty times as much as his salary, when he started out. It was still ten times as much, a couple of years ago."

"Boy . . . howdy." Castle was doing mental arithmetic and algebra with variables like Porsches and fast boats.

"But he let his sisters take care of it. He let them reinvest the capital."

"They weren't too swift?"

"They were idiots! They took good solid blue-chip stocks and tax-free municipals, too 'boring' for them, and threw it all away gambling on commodities." She grimaced. "*Pork* bellies? I finally had John go to Chicago and come back with what was left of his money. There wasn't much."

"You ain't broke, though."

"Damned near. There's enough income to pay for insurance, and eventually we'll be able to draw on an IRA. But the cash payments stop in two months. We'll have to live on John's salary. I suppose I'll get a job, too."

"What you ought to get is a typewriter."

Lena laughed and slouched back in her chair. "That would be something."

"You think he could do it? I mean, if he would, do you think he could?"

"He's a good writer." She looked thoughtful. "He's had some stories published, you know, in the literary magazines. The ones that pay four or five free copies."

"Big deal."

She shrugged. "Pays off in the long run. Tenure. But I don't know whether being able to write a good literary story means that John could write a good Hemingway imitation."

"He knows enough, right?"

"Maybe he knows too much. He might be paralyzed by his own standards." She shook her head. "In some ways he's an absolute nut about Hemingway. Obsessed, I mean. It's not good for him."

"Maybe writing this stuff would get it out of his system."

She smiled at him. "You've got more angles than a protractor."

"Sorry; I didn't mean to—"

"No." She raised both hands. "Don't be sorry; I like it. I like you, Castle. John's a good man, but sometimes he's too good."

He poured them both more wine. "Nobody ever accused me of that."

"I suspect not." She paused. "Have you ever been in trouble with the police? Just curious."

"Why?"

"Just curious."

He laughed. "Nickel and dime stuff, when I was a kid. You know, jus' to see what you can get away with." He turned serious. "Then I pulled two months' hard time for somethin' I didn't do. Wasn't even in town when it happened."

"What was it?"

"Armed robbery. Then the guy came back an' hit the same goddamn store! I mean, he was one sharp cookie. He confessed to the first one, and they let me go."

"Why did they accuse you in the first place?"

"Used to think it was somebody had it in for me. Like the

clerk who fingered me." He took a sip of wine. "But hell. It was just dumb luck. And dumb cops. The guy was about my height, same color hair, we both lived in the neighborhood. Cops didn't want to waste a lot of time on it. Jus' chuck me in jail."

"So you do have a police record?"

"Huh-uh. Girl from the ACLU made sure they wiped it clean. She wanted me to go after 'em for what, false arrest an' wrongful imprisonment. I just wanted to get out of town."

"It wasn't here?"

"Nah. Dayton, Ohio. Been here eight, nine years."

"That's good."

"Why the third degree?"

She leaned forward and patted the back of his hand. "Call it a job interview, Castle. I have a feeling we may be working together."

"Okay." He gave her a slow smile. "Anything else you want to know?"

---

5   The Doctor and the Doctor's Wife

John trudged into the kitchen the next morning, ignored the coffeepot, and pulled a green bottle of beer out of the fridge. He looked up at the skylight. Four scorpions, none of them moving. Have to call the bug man today.

Red wine hangover, the worst kind. He was too old for this. Cheap red wine hangover. He eased himself into a soft chair and carefully poured the beer down the side of the glass. Not too much noise, please.

When you drink too much, you ought to take a couple of aspirin, and some vitamins, and all the water you can hold, before retiring. If you drink too much, of course, you don't remember to do that.

The shower turned off with a bass clunk of plumbing. John winced and took a long drink, which helped a little. When he heard the bathroom door open, he called for Lena to bring the aspirin when she came out.

After a few minutes, she brought it out and handed it to him. "And how is Dr. Baird today?"

"Dr. Baird needs a doctor. Or an undertaker." He shook out two aspirin and washed them down with the last of the beer. "Like your outfit."

She was wearing only a towel around her head. She simpered and struck a dancer's pose and spun daintily around. "Think it'll catch on?"

"Oh my yes." At thirty-five, she still had the trim model's figure that had caught his eye in the classroom, fifteen years before. A safe, light tan was uniform all over her body, thanks to liberal use of sunblock and the private sunbathing area on top of the house—private except for the helicopter that came low overhead every weekday at one-fifteen. She always tried to be there in time to wave at it. The pilot had such white teeth. She wondered how many sunbathers were on his route.

She undid the towel and rubbed her long blond hair vigorously. "Thought I'd cool off for a few minutes before I got dressed. Too much wine, eh?"

"Couldn't you tell from my sparkling repartee last night?" He leaned back, eyes closed, and rolled the cool glass back and forth on his forehead.

"Want another beer?"

"Yeah. Coffee'd be smarter, though."

"It's been sitting all night."

"Pay for my sins." He watched her swivel lightly into the

kitchen and, more than ever before, felt the difference in their ages. Seventeen years; he was half again as old as she. A young man would say the hell with the hangover, go grab that luscious thing and carry her back to bed. The organ that responded to this meditation was his stomach, though, and it responded very audibly.

"Some toast, too. Or do you want something fancier?"

"Toast would be fine." Why was she being so nice? Usually if he drank too much, he reaped the whirlwind in the morning.

"Ugh." She saw the scorpions. "Five of them now."

"I wonder how many it will hold before it comes crashing down. Scorpions everywhere, stunned. Then angry."

"I'm sure the bug man knows how to get rid of them."

"In Africa they claimed that if you light a ring of fire around them with gasoline or lighter fluid, they go crazy, run amok, stinging themselves to death in their frenzies. Maybe the bug man could do that."

"Castle and I came up with a plan last night. It's kinda screwy, but it might just work."

"Read that in a book called *Jungle Ways*. I was eight years old and believed every word of it."

"We figured out a way that it would be legal. Are you listening?"

"Uh-huh. Let me have real sugar and some milk."

She poured some milk in a cup and put it in the microwave to warm. "Maybe we should talk about it later."

"Oh no. Hemingway forgery. You figured out a way to make it legal. Go ahead. I'm all ears."

"See, you tell the publisher first off what it is, that you wrote it and then had it typed up to look authentic."

"Sure, be a big market for that."

"In fact, there could be. You'd have to generate it, but it could happen." The toast sprang up, and she brought it and two cups of coffee into the living room on a tray. "See, the bogus manuscript is only one part of a book."

"I don't get it." He tore the toast into strips, to dunk in the strong Cuban coffee.

"The rest of the book is in the nature of an exegesis of your own text."

"If that con man knows what exegesis is, then I can crack a safe."

"That part's my idea. You're really writing a book *about* Hemingway. You use your own text to illustrate various points— 'I wrote it this way instead of that way because . . .' "

"It would be different," he conceded. "Perhaps the second most egotistical piece of Hemingway scholarship in history. A dubious distinction."

"You could write it tongue-in-cheek, though. It could be really amusing, as well as scholarly."

"God, we'd have to get an unlisted number, publishers calling us night and day. Movie producers. Might sell ten copies—if I bought nine."

"You really aren't getting it, John. You don't have a particle of larceny in your heart."

He put a hand on his heart and looked down. "Ventricles, auricles. My undying love for you, a little heartburn. No particles."

"See, you tell the publisher the truth . . . but the publisher doesn't have to tell the truth. Not until publication day."

"Okay. I still don't get it."

She took a delicate nibble of toast. "It goes like this. They print the bogus Hemingway up into a few copies of bogus bound galleys. Top secret."

"My exegesis carelessly left off."

"That's the ticket. They send it out to a few selected scholars, along with Xeroxes of a few sample manuscript pages. All they say, in effect, is 'Does this seem authentic to you? Please keep it under your hat, for obvious reasons.' Then they sit back and collect blurbs."

"I can see the kind of blurbs they'd get from Scott or Mike

or Jack, for instance. Some variation of 'What kind of idiot do you think I am?' "

"Those aren't the kind of people you send it to, dope! You send it to people who think they're experts, but aren't. Castle says this is how the Hitler thing almost worked—they knew better than to show it to historians in general. They showed it to a few people and didn't quote the ones who thought it was a fake. Surely you can come up with a list of people who would be easy to fool."

"Any scholar could. Be a different list for each one; I'd be on some of them."

"So they bring it out on April Fool's Day. You get the front page of the *New York Times Book Review*. *Publishers Weekly* does a story. Everybody wants to be in on the joke. Best-seller list, here we come."

"Yeah, sure, but you haven't thought it through." He leaned back, balancing the coffee cup on his slight potbelly. "What about the guys who give us the blurbs, those second-rate scholars? They're going to look pretty bad."

"We did think of that. No way they could sue, not if the letter accompanying the galleys is carefully written. It doesn't have to say—"

"I don't mean getting sued. I mean I don't want to be responsible for hurting other peoples' careers—maybe wrecking a career, if the person was too extravagant in his endorsement and had people looking for things to use against him. You know departmental politics. People go down the chute for less serious crimes than making an ass of themselves and their institution in print."

She put her cup down with a clatter. "You're always thinking about other people. Why don't you think about yourself for a change?" She was on the verge of tears. "Think about *us*."

"All right, let's do that. What do you think would happen to my career at BU if I pissed off the wrong people with this exercise? How long do you think it would take me to make full professor? Do you think BU would make a full professor out of a man who uses his specialty to pull vicious practical jokes?"

"Just do me the favor of thinking about it. Cool down and weigh the pluses and minuses. If you did it with the right touch, your department would love it—and God, Harry wants to get rid of the chairmanship so bad he'd give it to an ax murderer. You know you'll make full professor about thirty seconds before Harry hands you the keys to the office and runs."

"True enough." He finished the coffee and stood up in a slow creak. "I'll give it some thought. Horizontally." He turned toward the bedroom.

"Want some company?"

He looked at her for a moment. "Indeed I do."

---

6   In Those Days it Was No Uncommon Thing to Call a Man a Son of a Bitch

---

Castle was not a man inclined to modesty, and as he sat in Sloppy Joe's waiting for John and Lena to show up, he was very much in a self-congratulatory mood, not in the least aware that even this early in the game, the game had been taken from him. He had thought it up, but he was not in charge.

He was studying the yellowed newspaper photos of Hemingway on the wall behind him: Hemingway with big fish; Hemingway with dead lion; Hemingway looking intrepid in various wars. He had always thought the guy was kind of a blowhard, a real self-promoter, but he must have actually done some pretty dangerous things.

"Studying?" Lena slid into the chair across from him; John followed with three beers.

"He was a pretty brave guy, I guess."

" 'Fraid a nothin'," John quoted, and passed the beers around. "That's what he said when he was a baby. Some people claim he was a coward at heart, though, and only fought bulls and such to prove to himself over and over that he wasn't."

"Sounds kinda farfetched. You believe that?"

"I don't know. How could anybody know? He was a complicated man; you make some generalization about him and someone will always pop up with evidence to the contrary. What I hope is true is that the idea of fighting a bull or getting shot at scared him shitless, but he went ahead and did it anyhow."

"That'd make him more interesting."

"It would. Idiot heroes—every now and then in Vietnam you'd meet some guy who lacked the ability to visualize his own death. He'd do all sorts of audacious things. Maybe live through them. It wasn't bravery, though; just a lack of imagination."

"Any new thoughts about our little project?" Lena asked Castle.

"Checked up at the Hemingway House, and no dice. I saw two machines there, but no 1921 Corona."

"I was afraid that'd be too easy," John said. "Unlikely, too, since he'd gone through two wives and several books by the time he got here. Pauline probably wouldn't care to have him sitting there every day caressing the keys of a love gift from Hadley."

"So where you think it'd be?"

John shrugged. "Knowing Hemingway, he might have lost his temper and thrown it out of a window in Paris. Maybe *at* someone."

"Wait though," Lena said. "He did type the first book on it, the first real one, *The Sun Also Rises?*"

John got that walleyed look. "Yes. Typefaces match."

"Well, that was a best-seller; he was pretty famous after that. Surely he'd be smart enough not to just throw it away when he got a new one; he'd find some collector to pay good money for it."

"Sure he would," Castle said. "And it probably wound up in some museum by now. For the tax write-off."

"I don't know. Americans weren't as obsessed by famous people then, going through their garbage and all. He really might have just thrown it away, or given it to some other writer after he got a better one. He could be generous that way."

"Well, why don't we call up all these places you were talkin' about, in Montana and Boston and all. Ask if they've got the typewriter, and if they don't, where it might be at."

"I don't think so," Lena said. "The next year, then, this mysterious missing manuscript turns up . . ."

"Going to take more than a year," John said. "Someone might notice if I didn't show up for class."

"Well, however much time. The point is, we don't dare be too specific and certainly not too insistent. We don't want anybody to be able to put two and two together."

"How 'bout that place up in Boston, though? They probably got a list about where all the Hemingway junk is stored."

"Memorabilia. They may have."

"You were talkin' about goin' up there anyhow. Maybe it's time."

"Maybe it is," Lena said. "You could be doing all the style and format analysis and in the middle of some legitimate search request, say, 'By the way, is that typewriter still around anywhere?' "

"Get outa the heat, anyhow."

"You've never been to Boston in the summer. They can bake their beans on the sidewalk."

"Mother's been wanting to come down for a while. She's

been sort of pestering me, actually; you know how she likes Florida."

"Hmm. That's an idea. I could just say hello-goodbye and get on the plane." He found it hard to be in the same room with the woman for as much as an hour.

"It would be perfect. I'll just say you have to be out of town, so we'll have an extra bed for, how long?"

"Week, two weeks. Make it two weeks; I'll take the train back." John didn't mind flying, but he loved the rails, what was left of them.

Castle leaned back. "Yeah, I could make myself useful for a couple weeks, too. Like I was tellin' Lena, I'm pretty good with machines and things. In case we don't find that machine or like you say, the crazy son of a bitch threw it at somebody, I should get a couple old ones and take 'em apart. Sooner or later we'll find somebody's 1921 Corona and I'll be able to mess with it until it types like the real thing."

"That's excellent. Maybe you could find one up in Miami; if not, I'll try Boston. You could probably learn a lot from any old flea-market typewriter."

"I should practice typing on one, too," Lena said. "I haven't used anything but a word processor since high school."

"That's going to be frustrating, when it comes to typing the actual manuscript. One mistake and you'll have to start the page over—actually, a few words ex'ed out would be okay. But you'd have to follow his weird punctuation."

"You wouldn't have any samples, of course."

"Of course not. Why clutter up my files when my mind is already a hopeless mess? But you'll find a manuscript page from "Up in Michigan" following page fifty-seven of Berenson's *The Early Hemingway: A Stylistic Analysis*. Next to the couch. That's the right typewriter and the right period. In Boston, I'll send you copies of the whole story and some letters and whatnot."

Castle finished his beer and set down the glass. "Tell you what. I'll run up to Miami tomorrow and scout around. Maybe I can find an old machine that still has a repair manual."

"That would be good," John said. "Or maybe I could track down a manual in Boston."

Lena raised her glass in a toast. "Let's start tomorrow."

They clinked together. "Maybe I can be out of town before your mother gets here."

---

7   in our time

Back already?

Need to find a meta-causal. One guy seems to be generating the danger flag in various timelines. John Baird, who's a scholar in some of them, a soldier in some, and a rich playboy in a few. He's always a Hemingway nut, though. He does something that starts off the ripples in '95, '96, '97; depending on which timeline you're in—but I can't seem to get close to it. There's something odd about him, and it doesn't have to do with Hemingway specifically.

But he's definitely causing the eddy?

Has to be him.

All right. Find a meta-causal that all the doom lines have in common, and forget about the others. Then go talk to him.

There'll be resonance—

But who cares? Moot after AD 2006.

That's true. I'll hit all the doom lines at once, then: neutralize the meta-causal, then jump ahead and do some spot checks.

Good. And no killing this time.

I understand. But—

You're too close to 2006. Kill the wrong person and the whole thing could unravel.

*Well, there are differences of opinion. We would certainly feel it
if the world failed to come to an end in those lines.*

*As you say, differences of opinion. My opinion is that you better
not kill anybody or I'll send you back to patrol the fourteenth century
again.*

*Understood. But I can't guarantee that I can neutralize the
meta-causal without eliminating John Baird.*

*Fourteenth century. Some people love it. Others think it was
nasty, brutish, and long.*

---

8   Work in Progress

Harry Abramson was startled to see John Baird walk
through the office door. "Get too hot in Florida?"

"Worse here," he said, shaking hands. "Had to
come up and use the JFK Library a couple of days."

"That Hemingway collection?" He waved at a chair.

"Right." John sat down heavily. "Trying to finish a paper in
time to submit for next year's get-together in Nairobi."

"You guys pick the oddest places."

John nodded. "I also wanted to talk to you about, um, a
matter of ethics. Practical and theoretical."

The older man hesitated. "I'm an authority on that, of
course, as who isn't. What about?"

"It's crazy." He looked at his watch. "You have lunch
plans?"

He shrugged. "Dining hall."

"Let me save you from it."

"Great." Abramson thumbed an intercom and the secretary confirmed that he was free. "Nice there's one person in the department with some money." For two more months, John didn't say.

They walked to a new Italian place down by the bookstore. John picked at a cold pasta salad and explained the scheme in some detail, leaving Castle out of it.

Abramson was amused. "I see your problem. In some circles, it would look as if your main motivation would be to set up certain of your colleagues for ridicule."

"That's what I told Lena. It would make me look pretty mean-spirited."

"I don't know." He carefully bisected a last bit of veal. "I'm trying to think how I'd feel if it happened to me. Some publisher sends me galleys of a previously unknown Hawthorne, say, or Poe, along with a couple of manuscript pages—it would be a more difficult forgery, mind you, and therefore more convincing, since you'd have to duplicate the author's archaic handwriting with an archaic instrument—but suppose it was a good pastiche and I endorsed it.

"And so in the fullness of time it does come out, admitting itself to be a clever ruse, and there on the back cover is Professor Harry Abramson of Boston University saying 'A stunning discovery and an invaluable addition to the Poe canon.' "

He paused, tapping his fork against the plate, considering. "I suppose it would depend on what other people thought. If other people whose judgment I respected had also been taken in, I could live with it, and even be amused by it. If I stood alone on that book jacket, though, pilloried . . . I'd be ready to commit murder."

"A point well taken. It would be a mistake to be too selective . . . wait." He chuckled. "We could even make the endorsements an extension of the joke. Quote a number of people who weren't fooled by it, as well."

"No, no, no!" Abramson covered his eyes with a hand and

laughed. "You're not devious enough, John. Suppose we have this Poe forgery and there I am on the back cover saying it's the best thing since *The Fall of the House of Usher,* and right next to me is Paul Funderburk of Yale saying only an idiot would be taken in by this. You'd be asking for letter bombs." He shook his head. "How long have we known each other?"

"Oh boy. My second year in graduate school—call it twenty-five, twenty-six years, off and on."

"Right. And you're the last person in the world I would think of doing this. What is it, male menopause?"

"Just an attack of imagination. You see my problem, though. I really wouldn't want to hurt anybody by it. But it would be a pointless exercise if I didn't demonstrate that professionals could be fooled by it."

He nodded. "You know, if anybody could get away with it, come out unblemished, you could. Most people who would care know that you're in this business purely for the love of it. You're not out to make a fortune by trampling on people's reputations. Your atrocious sense of humor is well enough known, too."

The waiter came and took up their plates. "Maybe there's a way to defuse it. Try this on for size. You collect all these endorsements as if it were the real thing. But a couple of weeks before you go to press, you get back to all the people and tell them what the actual situation is. Ask whether they're willing to go along with the gag; show them a copy of the rest of the text. In the introduction, thank them for being good sports. A lot of people would go along with it—not everybody, and probably not the ones who would have made the most dramatic blurbs—but your posterior would be covered. Ethically speaking."

"God. Thanks, Harry. That's exactly what I'll do."

"You haven't asked the next question, though. Always ask the next question."

"Which is?"

"It goes like this: ethics or no ethics, what will this book do to my career? The answer is that it would probably sink you like a rock. This hypothetical guy who wrote the hypothetical Poe book would find himself grading freshman comp in a junior college in a state he'd never heard of." He sat back. "I wouldn't mind, but I'm not the one in charge of your advancement."

"I don't know, Harry. Hemingway scholars are a funny bunch. They might be inclined to forgive the joke and criticize the book in terms of its actual content."

Harry shook his head and laughed. "You know your people. They might surprise you, though." That was the last they said on the matter. Over coffee they discussed next semester's classes and the shortcomings of various people who were not present. Harry would of course keep mum about the joke; he was obviously flattered that John had taken him into his confidence.

When Harry went back to his office, John started for the Green Line, to go out to the Hemingway collection, but then turned around and headed the other way. By the time he could transfer twice and get to JFK there would only be a couple of hours before the collection closed; better to relax today and get an early start tomorrow.

Deep in thought, he crossed over the busy highway and down to the shady walk that curved alongside the Charles River. We do things for obscure reasons, he reflected. The actual motivation for talking to Harry was to make it impossible for him to do what Castle—and probably Lena—actually would want him to do: drop the amiable academic hoax and try to market the forgery for real. That would be impossible now.

Even if something happened to him, he thought with a delicious thrill. If life were a TV show, Castle and Lena would plot to dispose of him as soon as he'd finished the pastiche . . . no, they'd need his help in making the physical forgery convincing, too.

But not in marketing it. They could take it to any rare book dealer—or even straight to Sotheby's. Look at what I found in a safe in my late husband's office. No wonder he'd been so secretive since that last Paris trip . . .

Farfetched. But at least with Castle, some form of blackmail might materialize. So he would keep the meeting with Harry to himself for a while.

The water was too beautiful to ignore. He went back to his apartment and changed into jeans, then rented a Sunfish and sailed through the heat for a couple of hours in the wide basin between MIT and the Science Museum. It was relaxing and tiring; he ignored Boston's 2,136 restaurants and fixed dinner out of cans and fell asleep in front of the TV.

9   A Clean, Well-Lighted Place

Most of the sleuthing that makes up literary scholarship takes place in settings either neutral or unpleasant. Libraries' old stacks, attics metaphorical and actual; dust and silverfish, yellowed paper and fading ink. Books and letters that appear in card files but not on shelves.

Hemingway researchers have a haven outside of Boston, the Hemingway Collection at the University of Massachusetts's John F. Kennedy Library. It's a triangular room with one wall dominated by a picture window that looks over Boston Harbor to the sea. Comfortable easy chairs surround a coffee table, but John had never seen them in use; work tables under the picture window provided realistic room for computer and clutter. Skins from animals the Hemingways had dispatched in Africa snarled up from the floor, and one wall was dominated by Hemingway memorabilia and photographs. What made the room nirvana, though, was row upon row of boxes containing tens of thousands of Xeroxed pages of Hemingway correspondence, manuscripts, clippings—everything from a boyhood shopping list to all extant versions of every short story and poem and novel.

John liked to get there early so he could claim one of the three computers. He snapped it on, inserted a CD, and typed in his code number. Then he keyed in the data-base index and started searching.

The more commonly requested items would appear onscreen if you asked for them—whenever someone requested a physical copy of an item, an electronic copy automatically was sent into the data-base—but most of the things John needed were obscure, and he had to haul down the letter boxes and physically flip through them, just like some poor scholar inhabiting the first nine tenths of the twentieth century.

Time disappeared for him as he abandoned his notes and followed lines of instinct, leaping from letter to manuscript to note to interview, doing what was in essence the opposite of the scholar's job: a scholar would normally be trying to find out what these stories had been about. John, instead, was trying to track down every reference that might restrict what he himself could write about, simulating the stories.

The most confining restriction was the one he'd first remembered, walking away from the bar where he'd met Castle. The one-paragraph answer that Hadley had given to Carlos Baker about the unfinished novel; that it was a Nick Adams story about hunting and fishing up in Michigan. John didn't know anything about hunting, and most of his fishing experience was limited to watching a bobber and hoping it wouldn't go down and break his train of thought.

There was the one story that Hemingway had left unpublished, "Boys and Girls Together," mostly clumsy self-parody. It covered the right period and the right activities, but using it as a source would be sensitive business, tiptoeing through a mine field. Anyone looking for a fake would go straight there. Of course, John could go up to the Michigan woods and camp out, see things for himself and try to re-create them in the Hemingway style. Later, though. First order of business was to make sure there was nothing in this huge collection that would torpedo the whole project—some postcard where Hemingway said "You're going to like this novel because it has a big scene about cleaning fish."

The short stories would be less restricted in subject matter; according to Hemingway, they'd been about growing up in Oak Park and Michigan and the battlefields of Italy.

That made him stop and think. The one dramatic experience he shared with Hemingway was combat—fifty years later, to be sure, in Vietnam, but the basic situations couldn't have changed that much. Terror, heroism, cowardice. The guns and grenades were a little more streamlined, but they did the same things to people. Maybe do a World War I story as a finger exercise, see whether it would be realistic to try a longer growing-up-in-Michigan pastiche.

He made a note to himself about that on the computer, oblique enough not to be damning, and continued the eyestraining job of searching through Hadley's correspondence, trying to find some further reference to the lost novel—damn!

Writing to Ernest's mother, Hadley noted that "the taxi driver broke his typewriter" on the way to the Constantinople conference—did he get it fixed, or just chuck it? A quick check showed that the typeface of his manuscripts did indeed change after July, 1924. So they'd never be able to find it. There were typewriters in Hemingway shrines in Key West, Havana, Billings, Schruns; the initial plan had been to find which was the old Corona, then locate an identical one and have Castle arrange a swap.

So they would fall back on plan B. Castle had claimed to be good with mechanical things and thought if they could find a 1921 Corona, he could tweak the keys around so they would produce a convincing manuscript—lowercase *s* a hair low, *e* a hair high, and so forth. How he could be so sure of success without ever having seen the inside of a manual typewriter, John did not know. Nor did he have much confidence.

But it wouldn't have to be perfecct simulation, since they weren't out to fool the whole world, but just a few reviewers who would only see two or three Xeroxed pages. He could probably do a close enough job. John put it out of his mind and moved on to the next letter.

But it was an odd coincidence for him to think about Castle at that instant, since Castle was thinking about him. Or at least asking.

---

10 The Coming Man

"How was he when he was younger?"

"He never was younger." She laughed and rolled around inside the compass of his arms, to face him. "Than you, I mean. He was in his mid-thirties when we met. You can't be much over twenty-five."

He kissed the end of her nose. "Thirty this year. But I still get carded sometimes."

"I'm a year older than you are. So you have to do anything I say."

"So far so good." He'd checked her wallet when she'd gone into the bathroom to insert the diaphragm, and knew she was thirty-five. "Break out the whips and chains now?"

"Not till next week. Work up to it slowly." She pulled away from him and mopped her front with the sheet. "You're good at being slow."

"I like being asked to come back."

"How 'bout tonight and tomorrow morning?"

"If you feed me lots of vitamins. How long you think he'll be up in Boston?"

"He's got a train ticket for Wednesday. But he said he might stay longer if he got onto something."

Castle laughed. "Or into something. Think he might have a girl up there? Some student like you used to be?"

"That would be funny. I guess it's not impossible." She covered her eyes with the back of her hand. "The wife is always the last to know."

They both laughed. "But I don't think so. He's a sweet guy, but he's just not real sexy. I think his students see him as kind of a favorite uncle."

"You fell for him once."

"Uh-huh. He had all of his current virtues plus a full head of hair, no potbelly—and, hm, what am I forgetting?"

"He was hung like an elephant?"

"No, I guess it was the millions of dollars. That can be pretty sexy."

11   Wanderings

I t was a good thing John liked to nose around obscure neighborhoods shopping; you couldn't walk into any old K Mart and pick up a 1921 Corona portable. In fact, you couldn't walk into any typewriter shop in Boston and find one—not any. Nowadays they all sold self-contained word processors, with a few dusty old electrics in the back room. A few had fancy manual typewriters from Italy or Switzerland; it had been almost thirty years since the American manufacturers had made a machine that wrote without electronic help.

He had a little better luck with pawnshops. Lots of Smith-Coronas, a few L. C. Smiths, and two actual Coronas that might have been old enough. One had too large a typeface and the other, although the typeface was the same as Hemingway's, was missing a couple of letters: Th quick b own fox jump d ov   th lazy dog. The challenge of writing a convincing Hemingway novel without using the letters *e* and *r* seemed daunting. He bought the machine anyhow, thinking they might ultimately have two or several broken ones that could be concatenated into one reliable machine.

The old pawnbroker rang up his purchase and made change and slammed the cash drawer shut. "Now, you don't look to me like the kind of man who would hold it against a man who . . ." He shrugged. "Well, who sold you something and then suddenly remembered that there was a place with lots of those somethings?"

"Of course not. Business is business."

"I don't know the name of the guy or his shop; I think he

calls it a museum. Up in Brunswick, Maine. He's got a thousand old typewriters. He buys, sells, trades. That's the only place I know of you might find one with the missing whatever-you-call-ems."

"Fonts." He put the antique typewriter under his arm—the handle was missing—and shook the old man's hand. "Thanks a lot. This might save me weeks."

With some difficulty, John got together packing materials and shipped the machine to Key West, along with Xeroxes of a few dozen pages of Hemingway's typed copy and a note suggesting Castle see what he can do. Then he went to the library and found a Brunswick telephone directory. Under *Office Machines & Supplies* was listed Crazy Tom's Typewriter Museum and Sales Emporium. John rented a car and headed north.

The small town had rolled up its sidewalks by the time he got there. He drove past Crazy Tom's and pulled into the first motel. It had a neon VACANCY sign but the innkeeper had to be roused from a deep sleep. He took John's credit card number and directed him to room 14 and pointedly turned on the NO sign. There were only two other cars in the motel lot.

John slept late and treated himself to a full "trucker's" breakfast at the local diner: two pork chops and eggs and hash browns. Then he worked off ten calories by walking to the shop.

Crazy Tom was younger than John had expected, thirtyish, with an unruly shock of black hair. A manual typewriter lay upside down on an immaculate worktable, but most of the place was definitely maculate. Thousands of peanut shells littered the floor. Crazy Tom was eating them compulsively from a large wooden bowl. When he saw John standing in the doorway, he offered some. "Unsalted," he said. "Good for you."

John crunched his way over the peanut-shell carpet. The only light in the place was the bare bulb suspended over the worktable, though two unlit high-intensity lamps were clamped on either side of it. The walls were floor-to-ceiling gloomy shelves holding hundreds of typewriters, mostly black.

"Let me guess," the man said as John scooped up a handful

of peanuts. "You're here about a typewriter."

"A specific one. A 1921 Corona portable."

"Ah." He closed his eyes in thought. "Hemingway. His first. Or I guess the first after he started writing. A 'twenty-seven Corona—now, that'd be Faulkner."

"You get a lot of calls for them?"

"Couple times a year. People hear about this place and see if they can find one like the master used, whoever the master is to them. Sympathetic magic and all that. But you aren't a writer."

"I've had some stories published."

"Yeah, but you look too comfortable. You do something else. Teach school." He looked around in the gloom. "Corona Corona." Then he sang the six syllables to the tune of "Corrina, Corrina." He walked a few steps into the darkness and returned with a small machine and set it on the table. "Newer than 1920, because of the way it says *Corona* here. Older than 1927, because of the tab setup." He found a piece of paper and a chair. "Go on, try it."

John typed out a few quick foxes and aids to one's party. The typeface was identical to the one on the machine Hadley had given Hemingway before they'd been married. The up-and-down-displacements of the letters were different, of course, but Castle should be able to fix that once he'd practiced with the backup machine.

John cracked a peanut. "How much?"

"What you need it for?"

"Why is that important?"

"It's the only one I got. Rather rent it than sell it." He didn't look like he was lying, trying to push the price up. "A thousand to buy, a hundred a month to rent."

"Tell you what, then. I buy it, and if it doesn't bring me luck, you agree to buy it back at a pro ratum. My thousand dollars minus ten percent per month."

Crazy Tom stuck out his hand. "Let's have a beer on it."

"Isn't it a little early for that?"

"Not if you eat peanuts all morning." He took two long-necked Budweisers from a cooler and set them on paper towels on the table. "So what kind of stuff you write?"

"Short stories and some poetry." The beer was good after the heavy, greasy breakfast. "Nothing you would've seen unless you read magazines like *Iowa Review* and *Triquarterly*."

"Oh yeah. Foldouts of Gertrude Stein and H.R. I might've read your stuff."

"John Baird."

He shook his head. "Maybe. I'm no good with names."

"If you recognized my name from the *Iowa Review*, you'd be the first person who ever had."

"I was right about the Hemingway connection?"

"Of course."

"But you don't write like Hemingway for no *Iowa Review*. Short declarative sentences, truly this truly that."

"No, you were right about the teaching, too. I teach Hemingway up at Boston University."

"So that's why the typewriter? Play show-and-tell with your students?"

"That, too. Mainly I want to write some on it and see how it feels."

From the back of the shop, a third person listened to the conversation with great interest. He, it, wasn't really a person, though he could look like one: he had never been born and he would never die. But then he didn't really exist, not in the down-home pinch-yourself-ouch! way that you and I do. In another way, he did *more* than exist, since he could slip back and forth between places you and I don't even have words for.

He was carrying a wand that could be calibrated for heart attack, stroke, or metastasized cancer on one end; the other end induced a kind of aphasia. He couldn't use it unless he materialized. He walked toward the two men, making no crunching sounds on the peanut shells because he weighed less than a thought. He studied John Baird's face from about a foot away.

"I guess it's a mystical thing, though I'm uncomfortable

with that word. See whether I can get into his frame of mind."

"Funny thing," Crazy Tom said. "I never thought of him typing out his stories. He was always sitting in some café writing in notebooks, piling up saucers."

"You've read a lot about him?" That would be another reason not to try the forgery. This guy comes out of the woodwork and says "I sold John Baird a 1921 Corona portable."

"Hell, all I do is read. If I get two customers a day, one of 'em's a mistake and the other just wants directions. I've read all of Hemingway's fiction and most of the journalism and, I think, all of the poetry. Not just the *Querschnitt* period; the more interesting stuff."

The invisible man was puzzled. Quite obviously, John Baird planned some sort of Hemingway forgery. But then he should be growing worried over this man's dangerous expertise. Instead, he was radiating relief.

What course of action, inaction? He could go back a few hours in time and steal this typewriter, though he would have to materialize for that and it would cause suspicions. And Baird could find another. He could kill one or both of them, now or last week or next, but that would mean duty in the fourteenth century for more than forever—when you exist out of time, a century of unpleasantness is long enough for planets to form and die.

He wouldn't have been drawn to this meeting if it were not a strong causal nexus. There must be earlier ones, since John Baird did not just stroll down a back street in this little town and decide to change history by buying a typewriter. But the earlier ones must be too weak, or something was masking them.

Maybe it was a good timeplace to get John Baird alone and explain things to him. Then use the wand on him. But no, not until he knew exactly what he was preventing. With considerable effort of will and expenditure of something like energy, he froze time at this instant and traveled to a couple of hundred adjacent realities that were all in this same bundle of doomed timelines.

In most of them, Baird was here in Crazy Tom's Typewriter Museum and Sales Emporium. In some, he was in a similar place in New York. In two, he was back at the Hemingway Collection. In one, John Baird didn't exist: the whole planet was a lifeless blasted cinder. He'd known about that timeline; it had been sort of a dry run.

"He did both," John then said in most of the timelines. "Sometimes typing, sometimes fountain pen or pencil. I've seen the rough draft of his first novel. Written out in a stack of seven French schoolkids' copybooks." He looked around, memory working. A red herring wouldn't hurt. He'd never come across a reference to any other specific Hemingway typewriter, but maybe this guy had. "You know what kind of machine he used in Key West or Havana?"

Crazy Tom pulled on his chin. "Nope. Bring me a sample of the typing and I might be able to pin it down, though. And I'll keep an eye out—got a card?"

John took out a business card and his checkbook. "Take a check on a Boston bank?"

"Sure. I'd take one on a Tierra del Fuego bank. Who'd stiff you on a seventy-year-old typewriter?" Sylvester Castlemaine might, John thought. "I've had this business almost twenty years," Tom continued. "Not a single bounced check or bent plastic."

"Yeah," John said. "Why would a crook want an old typewriter?" The invisible man laughed and went away.

12 Banal Story

Dear Lena & Castle,

Typing this on the new/old machine to give you an idea about what has to be modified to mimic EH's:

abcdefghijklmnopqrstuvwxyz ABCDEFGHIJKLMNOPQRSTUVWXYZ

234567890,./ "#$%_&'()*?

Other mechanical things to think about --

1. Paper -- One thing that made people suspicious about the Hitler forgery is that experts know that old paper smells old. And of course there was that fatal chemical-composition error that clinched it.

As we discussed, my first thought was that one of us would have to go to Paris and nose around in old attics and so forth, trying to find either a stack of 75-year-old paper or an old blank book we could cut pages out of. But in the JFK Library collection I found out that EH actually did bring some American-made paper along with him. A lot of the rough draft of in our time -- written in Paris a year or two after our "discovery" -- was typed on the back of 6x7" stationery from his parents' vacation place in Windemere, Xerox enclosed. It should be pretty easy to duplicate on a hand press, and of course it will be a lot easier to find 75-year-old American paper. One complication, unfortunately, is that I haven't

really seen the paper; only a Xerox of the pages. Have to
come up with some pretext to either visit the vault or have
a page brought up, so I can check the color of the ink, mem-
orize the weight and deckle of the paper, check to see how the
edges are cut . . .

I'm starting to sound like a real forger. In for a penny,
though, in for a pound. One of the critics who's sent the
fragment might want to see the actual document, and compare it
with the existing Windemere pages.

2. Inks. This should not be a problem. Here's a recipe
for typewriter ribbon ink from a 1918 book of commercial form-
ulas:

8 oz. lampblack

4 oz. gum arabic

1 quart methylated spirits

That last one is wood alcohol. The others ought to be
available in Miami if you can't find them on the Rock.

Aging the ink on the paper gets a little tricky. I
haven't been able to find anything about it in the libraries
around here; no FORGERY FOR FUN & PROFIT. May check in New
York before coming back.

(If we don't find anything, I'd suggest baking it for a
few days at a temperature low enough not to greatly affect the
paper, and then interleaving it with blank sheets of the old
paper and pressing them together for a few days, to restore the
old smell, and further absorb the residual ink solvents.)

Toyed with the idea of actually allowing the manuscript to mildew somewhat, but that might get out of hand and actually destroy some of it -- or for all I know we'd be employing a species of mildew that doesn't speak French. Again, thinking like a true forger, which may be a waste of time and effort, but I have to admit is kind of fun. Playing cops and robbers at my age.

Well, I'll call tonight. Miss you, Lena.

Your partner in crime,

John.

---

13   A Divine Gesture

When John returned to his place in Boston, there was a message on his answering machine: "John, this is Nelson Van Nuys. Harry told me you were in town. I left something in your box at the office and I strongly suggest you take it before somebody else does. I'll be out of town for a week, but give me a call if you're here next Friday. You can take me and Doris out to dinner at Panache."

Panache was the most expensive restaurant in Cambridge. Interesting. John checked his watch. He hadn't planned to go to the office, but there was plenty of time to swing by on his way to returning the rental car. The train didn't leave for another four hours.

Van Nuys was a fellow Hemingway scholar and sometimes drinking buddy who taught at Brown. What had he brought fifty miles to deliver in person, rather than mail? He was probably just in town and dropped by. But it was worth checking.

No one but the secretary was in the office, noontime, for which John was obscurely relieved. In his box were three inter-departmental memos, a textbook catalog, and a brown cardboard box that sloshed when he picked it up. He took it all back to his office and closed the door.

The office made him feel a little weary, as usual. He wondered whether they would be shuffling people around again this year. The department liked to keep its professors in shape by having them haul tons of books and files up and down the corridor every couple of years.

He glanced at the memos and pitched them, irrelevant since he wasn't teaching in the summer, and put the catalog in his briefcase. Then he carefully opened the cardboard box.

It was a half-pint Jack Daniel's bottle, but it didn't have bourbon in it. A cloudy greenish liquid. John unscrewed the top and with the sharp Pernod tang the memory came back: he and Van Nuys had wasted half an afternoon in Paris years ago, trying to track down a source of true absinthe. So he had finally found some.

Absinthe. Nectar of the gods, ruination of several genera-tions of French artists, students, workingmen—outlawed in 1915 for its addictive and hallucinogenic qualities. Where had Van Nuys found it?

He screwed the top back on tightly and put it back in the box and put the box in his briefcase. If its effect really was all that powerful, you probably wouldn't want to drive under its influ-ence. In Boston traffic, of course, a little lane weaving and a few mild collisions would go unnoticed.

Once he was safely on the train, he'd try a shot or two of it. It couldn't be all that potent. Child of the sixties, John had taken LSD, psilocybin, ecstasy, and peyote, and remembered with complete accuracy the quality of each drug's hallucinations.

The effects of absinthe wouldn't be nearly as extreme as its modern successors. But it was probably just as well to try it first in a place where unconsciousness or Steve Allen imitations or speaking in tongues would go unremarked.

He turned in the rental car and took a cab to South Station rather than juggle suitcase, briefcase, and typewriter through the subway system. Once there, he nursed a beer through an hour of the Yankees' murdering the Red Sox, and then rented a cart to roll his burden down to track 3, where a smiling porter installed him aboard the *Silver Meteor*, its range newly extended from Boston to Miami.

He had loved the train since his boyhood in Washington. His mother hated flying and so they often clickety-clacked from place to place in the snug comfort of first-class compartments. Eidetic memory blunted his enjoyment of the modern Amtrak version. This compartment was as large as the ones he had read and done puzzles in, forty years before—but the smell of good old leather was gone, replaced by plastic, and the fittings that had been polished brass were chromed steel now. On the middle of the red plastic seat was a Hospitality Pak, a plastic box encased in plastic wrap that contained a wedge of indestructible "cheese food," as if cheese had to eat, a small plastic bottle of cheap California wine, a plastic glass to contain it, and an apple, possibly not plastic.

John hung up his coat and tie in the small closet provided beside where the bed would fold down, and for a few minutes he watched with interest as his fellow passengers and their accompaniment hurried or ambled to their cars. Mostly old people, of course. Enough young ones, John hoped, to keep the trains alive a few decades more.

"Mr. Baird?" John turned to face a black porter, who bowed slightly and favored him with a blinding smile of white and gold. "My name is George and I will be at your service as far as Atlanta. Is everything satisfactory?"

"Doing fine. But if you could find me a glass made of glass and a couple of ice cubes, I might mention you in my will."

"One minute, sir." In fact, it took less than a minute. That was one aspect, John had to admit, that had improved in recent years: the service on Amtrak in the sixties and seventies had been right up there with Alcatraz and the Hanoi Hilton.

He closed and locked the compartment door and carefully poured about two ounces of the absinthe into the glass. Like Pernod, it turned milky on contact with the ice.

He swirled it around and breathed deeply. It did smell much like Pernod, but with an acrid tang that was probably oil of wormwood. An experimental sip: the wormwood didn't dominate the licorice flavor, but it was there.

"Thanks, Nelson," he whispered, and drank the whole thing in one cold fiery gulp. He set down the glass and the train began to move. For a weird moment that seemed hallucinatory, but it always did, the train starting off smoothly and silently.

For about ten minutes he felt nothing unusual, as the train did its slow tour of Boston's least attractive backyards. The conductor who checked his ticket seemed like a normal human being, which could have been a hallucination.

John knew that some drugs, like amyl nitrite, hit with a swift slap, while others creep into your mind like careful infiltrators. This was the way of absinthe; all he felt was a slight alcohol buzz, and he was about to take another shot, when it subtly began.

There were *things* just at the periphery of his vision, odd things with substance but somehow without shape, that of course moved away when he turned his head to look at them. At the same time a whispering began in his ears, just audible over the train noise, but not intelligible, as if in a language he had heard before but not understood. For some reason the effects were pleasant, though of course they could be frightening if a person were not expecting weirdness. He enjoyed the illusions for a few minutes, while the scenery outside mellowed into woodsy suburbs, and the visions and voices stopped rather suddenly.

He poured another ounce and this time diluted it with water. He remembered the sad woman in "Hills Like White

Elephants" lamenting that everything new tasted like licorice, and allowed himself to wonder what Hemingway had been drinking when he wrote that curious story.

Chuckling at his own—what? effrontery?—John took out the 1921 Corona and slipped a sheet of paper into it and balanced it on his knees. He had earlier thought of the first two lines of the WWI pastiche; he typed them down and kept going:

```
The dirt on the sides of the trenches was never completely
dry in the morning. If Nick could find an old newspaper he
would put it between his chest and the dirt when he went out to
lean on the side of the trench and wait for the light. First
light was the best time. You might have luck and see a muzzle
flash. But patience was better than luck. Wait to see a hel-
met or a head without a helmet.

Nick looked at the enemy line through a rectangular box of
wood that went through the trench at about ground level. The
other end of the box was covered by a square of gauze the color
of dirt. A person looking directly at it might see the muzzle
flash when Nick fired through the box. But with luck, the
flash would be the last thing he saw.

Nick had fired through the gauze six times, perhaps
killing three enemy, and the gauze now had a ragged hole in
the center.
```

Okay, John thought, he'd be able to see slightly better through the hole in the center, but staring that way would reduce the effective field of view, so he would deliberately try to look to one side or the other. How to type that down in a simple way? Someone cleared his throat.

John looked up from the typewriter. Sitting across from him was Ernest Hemingway, the weathered, wise Hemingway of the famous Karsh photograph. "I'm afraid you must not do that," Hemingway said.

John looked at the half-full glass of absinthe and looked back. Hemingway was still there. "Jesus Christ," he said.

"It isn't the absinthe." Hemingway's image rippled and he became the handsome teenager who had gone to war, the war John was writing about. "I am quite real. In a way, I am more real than you are." As it spoke it aged: the mustachioed leading-man-handsome Hemingway of the twenties; the slightly corpulent, still magnetic media hero of the thirties and forties; the beard turning white, the features hard and sad and then twisting with impotence and madness, and finally a sudden loud report and the cranial vault exploding, blood and brains splashing the mahogany veneer of the wall. Light glittered off embedded chips of skull. There was a strong smell of cordite and blood. The almost headless corpse shrugged, spreading its hands, one of which held a smoking shotgun. "I can look like anyone I want." The mess disappeared and it became the young Hemingway again. The shotgun became an odd cane, half white and half black.

John slumped and stared.

"This thing you just started must never be finished. This Hemingway pastiche. It will ruin something very important."

"What could it ruin? I'm not even planning to—"

"Your plans are immaterial. If you continue with this project, it will profoundly affect the future."

"You're from the future?"

"I'm from the future and the past and other temporalities that you can't comprehend. But all you need to know is that you must not write this Hemingway story. If you do, I or someone like me will have to kill you."

It spun the cane around and tapped John's knee with the white end. There was a slight tingle.

"Now you won't be able to tell anybody about me, or write anything about me down. If you try to talk about me, the memory will disappear—and reappear moments later, along with the knowledge that I will kill you if you don't cooperate." It turned into the bloody corpse again. "Understood?"

"Of course."

"If you behave, you will never have to see me again." It started to fade.

"Wait. What do you really look like?"

"This . . ." For a few seconds John stared at an ebony presence deeper than black, at once points and edges and surfaces and volume and hints of further dimensions. "You can't really see or know," a voice whispered inside his head. He reached into the blackness and jerked his hand back, rimed with frost and numb. The thing disappeared.

He stuck his hand under his armpit and, after a few seconds, feeling returned. That last apparition was the unsettling one. He had Hemingway's appearance at every age memorized, and had seen the corpse in his mind's eye often enough. A drug could conceivably have brought them all together and made up this fantastic demand—which might actually be nothing more than a reasonable side of his nature trying to make him stop wasting time on this chancy and unscrupulous project.

But that thing. His hand was back to normal. Maybe a drug could do that, too; make your hand feel freezing. LSD did more profound things than that. But not while arguing about a manuscript.

He considered the remaining absinthe. Maybe take another big blast of it and see whether ol' Ernie comes back again. Or no—there was a simpler way to check.

The bar was four rocking and rolling cars away, and bouncing his way from wall to window helped sober John up. When he got there, he had another twinge for the memories of the past. Stained Formica tables. No service; you had to go to a bar at the other end. Acrid with cigarette fume. He remembered linen tablecloths and endless bottles of Coke with the names of cities from everywhere stamped on the bottom and, when his father came along with them, the rich sultry smoke of his Havanas.

The fat Churchills from Punch that emphysema stopped just before Castro could. "A Coke, please." He wondered which depressed him more, the red can or the plastic cup with miniature ice cubes.

The test. It was not in his nature to talk to strangers on public conveyances. But this was necessary. There was a man sitting alone who looked about John's age, a Social Security-bound hippy with wire-rim John Lennon glasses, white hair down to his shoulders, bushy gray beard. He nodded when John sat down across from him, but didn't say anything. He sipped beer and looked blankly out at the gathering darkness.

"Excuse me," John said, "but I have a strange thing to ask you."

The man looked at him. "I don't mind strange things. But please don't try to sell me anything illegal."

"I wouldn't. It may have something to do with a drug, but it would be one I took."

"You do look odd. You tripping?"

"Doesn't feel like it. But I may have been . . . slipped something." He leaned back and rubbed his eyes. "I just talked to Ernest Hemingway."

"The writer?"

"In my roomette, yeah."

"Wow. He must be pretty old."

"He's dead! More than thirty years."

"Oh wow. Now that is something weird. What he say?"

"You know what a pastiche is?"

"French pastry?"

"No, it's when you copy . . . when you create an imitation of another person's writing. Hemingway's, in this case."

"Is that legal? I mean, with him dead and all."

"Sure it is, as long as you don't try to foist it off as Hemingway's real stuff."

"So what happened? He wanted to help you with it?"

"Actually, no . . . he said I'd better stop."

"Then you better stop. You don't fuck around with ghosts."

He pointed at the old brass bracelet on John's wrist. "You in the 'Nam."

" 'Sixty-eight," John said. "Hue."

"Then you oughta know about ghosts. You don't fuck with ghosts."

"Yeah." What he'd thought was aloofness in the man's eyes, the set of his mouth, was aloneness, something slightly different. "You okay?"

"Oh yeah. Wasn't for a while, then I got my shit together." He looked out the window again, and said something weirdly like Hemingway: "I learned to take it a day at a time. The day you're in's the only day that's real. The past is shit and the future, hell, someday your future's gonna be that you got no future. So fuck it, you know? One day at a time."

John nodded. "What outfit were you in?"

"Like I say, man, the past is shit. No offense?"

"No, that's okay." He poured the rest of his Coke over the ice and stood up to go.

"You better talk to somebody about those ghosts. Some kinda shrink, you know? It's not that they're not real. But just you got to deal with 'em."

"Thanks. I will." John got a little more ice from the barman and negotiated his way down the lurching corridor back to his compartment, trying not to spill his drink while also juggling fantasy, reality, past, present, memory . . .

He opened the door and Hemingway was there, drinking his absinthe. He looked up with weary malice. "Am I going to have to kill you?"

What John did next would have surprised Castlemaine, who thought he was a nebbish. He closed the compartment door and sat down across from the apparition. "Maybe you can kill me and maybe you can't."

"Don't worry. I can."

"You said I wouldn't be able to talk to anyone about you. But I just walked down to the bar car and did."

"I know. That's why I came back."

"So if one of your powers doesn't work, maybe another doesn't. At any rate, if you kill me you'll never find out what went wrong."

"That's very cute, but it doesn't work." It finished off the absinthe and then ran a finger around the rim of the glass, which refilled out of nowhere.

"You're making assumptions about causality that are necessarily naive, because you can't perceive even half of the dimensions that you inhabit."

"Nevertheless, you haven't killed me yet."

"And assumptions about my 'psychology' that are absurd. I am no more a human being than you are a paramecium."

"I'll accept that. But I would make a deal with a paramecium if I thought I could gain an advantage from it."

"What could you possibly have to deal with, though?"

"I know something about myself that you evidently don't, that enables me to overcome your don't-talk restriction. Knowing that might be worth a great deal to you."

"Maybe something."

"What I would like in exchange is, of course, my life, and an explanation of why I must not do the Hemingway pastiche. Then I wouldn't do it."

"You wouldn't do it if I killed you, either."

John sipped his Coke and waited.

"All right. It goes something like this. There is not just one universe, but actually uncountable zillions of them. They're all roughly the same size and complexity as this one, and they're all going off in a zillion different directions, and it is one hell of a job to keep things straight."

"You do this by yourself? You're God?"

"There's not just one of me. In fact, it would be meaningless to assign a number to us, but I guess you could say that altogether, we are God . . . and the Devil, and the Cosmic Puppet Master, and the Grand Unification Theory, the Great Pumpkin and everything else. When we consider ourselves as a group, let me see, I suppose a human translation of our name would be the Spacio-Temporal Adjustment Board."

"STAB?"

"I guess that is unfortunate. Anyhow, what STAB does is more the work of a scalpel than a knife." The Hemingway scratched its nose, leaving the absinthe suspended in midair. "Events are supposed to happen in certain ways, in certain sequences. You look at things happening and say cause-and-effect, or coincidence, or golly, that couldn't have happened in a million years—but you don't even have a clue. Don't even try to think about it. It's like an ant trying to figure out General Relativity."

"It wouldn't have a clue. Wouldn't know where to start."

The apparition gave him a sharp look and continued. "These universes come in bundles. Hundreds of them, thousands, that are pretty much the same. And they affect each other. Resonate with each other. When something goes wrong in one, it resonates and screws up all of them."

"You mean to say that if I write a Hemingway pastiche, hundreds of universes are going to go straight to hell?"

The apparition spread its hands and looked to the ceiling. "Nothing is simple. The only thing that's simple is that nothing is simple.

"I'm a sort of literature specialist. American literature of the nineteenth and twentieth centuries. Usually. Most of my timespace is taken up with guys like Hemingway, Teddy Roosevelt, Heinlein, Bierce. Crane, Spillane, Twain."

"Not William Dean Howells?"

"Not him or James or Carver or Coover or Cheever or any of those guys. If everybody gave me as little trouble as William Dean Howells, I could spend most of my timespace on a planet where the fishing was good."

"Masculine writers?" John said. "But not all hairy-chested macho types."

"I'll give you an A minus on that one. They're writers who have an accumulating effect on the masculine side of the American national character. There's no one word for it, though it is a specific thing: individualistic, competence-worshiping, short-term optimism and long-term existentialism. 'There may be nothing after I die but I sure as hell will do the job right while I'm here, even though I'm surrounded by idiots.' You see the pattern?"

"Okay. And I see how Hemingway fits in. But how could writing a pastiche interfere with it?"

"That's a limitation I have. I don't know specifically. I do know that the accelerating revival of interest in Hemingway from the seventies through the nineties is vitally important. In the Soviet Union as well as the United States. For some reason, I can feel your pastiche interfering with it." He stretched out the absinthe glass into a yard-long amber crystal, and it changed into the black-and-white cane. The glass reappeared in the drink holder by the window. "Your turn."

"You won't kill me after you hear what I have to say?"

"No. Go ahead."

"Well . . . I have an absolutely eidetic memory. Everything I've ever seen—or smelled or tasted or heard or touched, or even dreamed—I can instantly recall.

"Every other memory freak I've read about was limited—numbers, dates, calendar tricks, historical details—and most of them were *idiots savants*. I have at least normal intelligence. But from the age of about three, I have never forgotten anything."

The Hemingway smiled congenially. "Thank you. That's exactly it." It fingered the black end of the cane, clicking something. "If you had the choice, would you rather die of a heart attack, stroke, or cancer?"

"That's it?" The Hemingway nodded. "Well, you're human enough to cheat. To lie."

"It's not something you could understand. Stroke?"

"It might not work."

"We're going to find out right now." He lowered the cane.

"Wait! What's death? Is there . . . anything I should do, anything you know?"

The rod stopped, poised an inch over John's knee. "I guess you just end. Is that so bad?"

"Compared to not ending, it's bad."

"That shows how little you know. I and the ones like me can never die. If you want something to occupy your last moment, your last thought, you might pity me."

John stared straight into his eyes. "*Fuck* you."

The cane dropped. A fireball exploded in his head.

---

14 Marriage is a Dangerous Game

"We'll blackmail him." Castle and Lena were together in the big antique bathtub, in a sea of pink foam, her back against his chest.

"Sure," she said. " 'If you don't let us pass this manuscript off as the real thing, we'll tell everybody you faked it.' Something wrong with that, but I can't quite put my finger on it."

"Here, I'll put mine on it."

She giggled. "Later. What do you mean, blackmail?"

"Got it all figured out. I've got this friend Pansy; she used to be a call girl. Been out of the game seven, eight years; still looks like a million bucks."

"Sure. We fix John up with this hooker—"

"Call girl isn't a hooker. We're talkin' class."

"In the first place, John wouldn't pay for sex. He did that in Vietnam and it still bothers him."

"Not talkin' about pay. Talkin' about fallin' in love. While she meanwhile fucks his eyeballs out."

"You have such a turn of phrase, Sylvester. Then while his eyeballs are out, you come in with a camera."

"Yeah, but you're about six steps ahead."

"Okay, step two—how do we get them together? Church social?"

"She moves in next door." There was another upstairs apartment, unoccupied. "You and me and Julio are conveniently somewhere else when she shows up with all these boxes and that big flight of stairs."

"Sure, John would help her. But that's his nature; he'd help her if she were an ugly old crone with leprosy. Carry a few boxes, sit down for a cup of coffee, maybe. But not jump into the sack."

"Okay, you know John." His voice dropped to a husky whisper and he cupped her breasts. "But I know men, and I know Pansy . . . and Pansy could give a hard-on to a corpse."

"Sure, and then fuck his eyeballs out. They'd come out easier."

"What?"

"Never mind. Go ahead."

"Well . . . look. Do you know what a call girl does?"

"I suppose you call her up and say you've got this eyeball problem."

"Enough with the eyeballs. What she does, she works for, like, an escort service. That part of it's legal. Guy comes into town, business or maybe on vacation, he calls up the service and they ask what kind of companion he'd like. If he says, like, give me some broad with a tight ass, can suck the chrome off a bumper hitch—the guy says, like, 'I'm sorry, sir, but this is not that kind of a service.' But mostly the customers are pretty hip to it, they say, oh, a pretty young blonde who likes to go dancing."

"Meanwhile they're thinking about bumper hitches and eyeballs."

"You got it. So it starts out just like a date, just the guy pays the escort service, like, twenty bucks for getting them together. Still no law broken."

"Now about one out of three, four times, that's it. The guy knows what's going on but he don't get up the nerve to ask, or he really doesn't know the score, and it's, like, a real dull date. I don't think that happened much with Pansy."

"In the normal course of things, though, the subject of bumper hitches comes up."

"Uh-huh, but not from Pansy. The guy has to pop the question. That way if he's a cop it's, what, entrapment."

"Do you know whether Pansy ever got busted?"

"Naw. Mainly the cops just shake down the hookers, just want a blow job anyhow. This town, half of 'em want a blow job from guys."

"So they pop the question and Pansy blushes and says for you, I guess I could. Then on the way to the motel or wherever she says, you know, I wouldn't ask this if we weren't really good friends, but I got to make a car payment by tomorrow, and I need, like, two hundred bucks before noon tomorrow."

"And she takes MasterCard and Visa."

"No, but she sure as hell knows where every bank machine in town is. She even writes up an IOU." Castle laughed. "Told me a guy from Toledo's holdin' five grand of IOUs from her."

"All right, but that's not John. She could suck the chrome off his eyeballs and he still wouldn't be interested in her if she didn't know Hemingway from hummingbirds."

Castle licked behind her ear, a weird gesture that made her shiver. "That's the trump card. Pansy reads like a son of a bitch. She's got, like, a thousand books. So this morning I called her up and asked about Hemingway."

"And?"

"She's read them *all*."

She nodded slowly. "Not bad, Sylvester. So we promote this love affair and sooner or later you catch them in the act. Threaten to tell me unless John accedes to a life of crime."

"Think it could work? He wouldn't say, Hell, go ahead and tell her?"

"Not if I do my part . . . starting tomorrow; I'm the best, sweetest, lovingest wife in this sexy town. Then in a couple of weeks Pansy comes into his life, and there he is, luckiest man alive. Best of both worlds. Until you accidentally catch them *in flagrante delicioso*."

"So to keep both of you, he goes along with me."

"It might just do it. It might just." She slowly levered herself out of the water and smoothed the suds off her various assets.

"Nice."

"Bring me that bumper hitch, Sylvester. Hold on to your eyeballs."

---

15   In Another Country

J ohn woke up with a hangover of considerable dimension. The diluted glass of absinthe was still in the drink holder by the window. It was just past dawn, and a verdant forest rushed by outside. The rails made a steady hum; the car had a slight rocking that would have been pleasant to a person who felt well.

A porter knocked twice and inquired after Mr. Baird. "Come in," John said. A short white man, smiling, brought in coffee and danish.

"What happened to George?"

"Pardon me, sir? George who?"

John rubbed his eyes. "Oh, of course. We must be past Atlanta."

"No, sir." The man's smile froze as his brain went into nutty-passenger mode. "We're at least two hours from Atlanta."

"George . . . is a tall black guy with gold teeth who—"

"Oh, you mean George Mason, sir. He does do this car, but he picks up the train in Atlanta, and works it to Miami and back. He hasn't had the northern leg since last year."

John nodded slowly and didn't ask what year it was. "I understand." He smiled up and read the man's name tag. "I'm sorry, Leonard. Not at my best in the morning." The man withdrew with polite haste.

Suppose that weird dream had not been a dream. The Hemingway creature had killed him—the memory of the stroke was awesomely strong and immediate—but all that death amounted to was slipping into another universe where George Mason was on a different shift. Or perhaps John had gone completely insane.

The second explanation seemed much more reasonable.

On the tray underneath the coffee, juice, and danish was a copy of *USA Today*, a paper John normally avoided because, although it had its comic aspects, it didn't have any funnies. He checked the date, and it was correct. The news stories were plausible—wars and rumors of war—so at least he hadn't slipped into a dimension where Martians ruled an enslaved Earth or Barry Manilow was president. He turned to the weather map and stopped dead.

Yesterday the country was in the middle of a heat wave that had lasted weeks. It apparently had ended overnight. The entry for Boston, yesterday, was 72/58/sh. But it hadn't rained, and the temperature had been in the nineties.

He went back to the front page and began checking news stories. He didn't normally pay much attention to the news, though, and hadn't seen a paper in several days. They'd canceled their *Globe* delivery for the six weeks in Key West, and he hadn't been interested enough to go seek out a newsstand.

There was no mention of the garbage collectors' strike in New York; he'd overheard a conversation about that yesterday. A long obituary for a rock star he was sure had died the year before.

An ad for De Soto automobiles. That company had gone out of business when he was a teenager.

Bundles of universes, different from each other in small ways. Instead of dying, or maybe because of dying, he had slipped into another one. What would be waiting for him in Key West? Maybe John Baird.

He set the tray down and hugged himself, trembling. Who or what was he in this universe? All of his memories, all of his personality, were from the one he had been born in. What happened to the John Baird that was born in this one? Was he an associate professor in American literature at Boston University? Was he down in Key West wrestling with a paper to give at Nairobi—or working on a forgery? Or was he a Fitzgerald specialist snooping around the literary attics of St. Paul, Minnesota?

The truth came suddenly. Both John Bairds were in this compartment, in this body. And the body was slightly different.

He opened the door to the small washroom and looked in the mirror. His hair was a little shorter, less gray, beard better trimmed.

He was less paunchy and . . . something felt odd. There was feeling in his thigh. He lowered his pants and there was no scar where the sniper bullet had opened his leg and torn up the nerves there.

That was the touchstone. As he raised his shirt, the parallel memory flooded in. Puckered round scar on the abdomen; in this universe the sniper had hit a foot higher—and instead of the convalescent center in Cam Ranh Bay, the months of physical therapy and then back into the war, it had been peritonitis raging; surgery in Saigon and Tokyo and Walter Reed, and no more army.

But slowly they converged again. Amherst and U. Mass—perversely using the GI bill in spite of his access to millions—the doctorate on *The Sun Also Rises* and the instructorship at BU, meeting Lena and virtuously waiting until after the semester to ask her out. Sex on the second date and the third . . . but there they verged again. This John Baird hadn't gone back into combat to have his midsection sprayed with shrapnel from an American grenade that bounced off a tree; never had dozens of bits of metal cut out of his dick—and in the ensuing twenty-five years had made more use of it. Girlfriends and even one disastrous homosexual encounter with a stranger. As far as he knew, Lena was in the dark about this side of him; thought that he had remained faithful other than one incident seven years after they married. He knew of one affair she had had with a colleague, and suspected more.

The two Johns' personalities and histories merged, separate but one, like two vines from a common root, climbing a single support.

Schizophrenic but not insane.

John looked into the mirror and tried to address his new or his old self—John-one, John-two. There were no such people. There was suddenly a man who had existed in two separate universes and, in a way, it was no more profound than having lived in two separate houses.

The difference being that nobody else knows there is more than one house.

He moved over to the window and set his coffee in the holder; picked up the absinthe glass and sniffed it, considered pouring it down the drain, but then put it in the other holder, for possible future reference.

Posit this: is it more likely that there are bundles of parallel universes prevailed over by a Hemingway lookalike with a magic cane, or that John Baird was exposed to a drug that he had never experienced before and it had had an unusually disorienting effect?

He looked at the paper. He had not hallucinated two weeks of drought. The rock star had been dead for some time. He had not seen a De Soto in twenty years, and that was a hard car to miss. Tailfins that had to be registered as lethal weapons.

But maybe if you take a person who remembers every trivial thing and zap his brain with oil of wormwood, that is exactly the effect: perfectly recalled things that never actually happened.

The coffee tasted repulsive. John put on a fresh shirt and decided not to shave and headed for the bar car. He bought the last imported beer in the cooler and sat down across from the long-haired, white-bearded man who had an earring that had escaped his notice before, or hadn't existed in the other universe.

The man was staring out at the forest greening by. "Morning," John said.

"How do." The man looked at him with no sign of recognition.

"Did we talk last night?"

He leaned forward. "What?"

"I mean did we sit in this car last night and talk about Hemingway and Vietnam and ghosts?"

He laughed. "You're on somethin', man. I been on this train since two in the mornin' and ain't said boo to nobody but the bartender."

"You were in Vietnam?"

"Yeah, but that's over; that's shit." He pointed at John's bracelet. "What, you got ghosts from over there?"

"I think maybe I have."

He was suddenly intense. "Take my advice, man; I been there. You got to go talk to somebody. Some shrink. Those ghosts ain't gonna go 'way by themself."

"It's not that bad."

"It ain't the ones you killed." He wasn't listening. "Fuckin' dinks, they come back but they don't, you know, they just stand around." He looked at John and tears came so hard they actually spurted from his eyes. "It's your fuckin' friends, man, they all died and they come back now . . ." He took a deep breath and wiped his face. "They use to come back every night. That like you?" John shook his head, helpless, trapped by the man's grief. "Every fuckin' night, my old lady, finally she said you go to a shrink or go to hell." He fumbled with the button on his shirt pocket and took out a brown plastic prescription bottle and stared at the label. He shook out a capsule. "Take a swig?" John pushed the beer over to him. He washed the pill down without touching the bottle to his lips.

He sagged back against the window. "I musta not took the pill last night, sometimes I do that. Sorry." He smiled weakly. "One day at a time, you know? You get through the one day. Fuck the rest. Sorry." He leaned forward again suddenly and put his hand on John's wrist. "You come outa nowhere and I lay my fuckin' trip on you. You don't need it."

John covered the hand with his own. "Maybe I do need it. And maybe I didn't come out of nowhere." He stood up. "I will see somebody about the ghosts. Promise."

"You'll feel better. It's no fuckin' cure-all but you'll feel better."

"Want the beer?"

He shook his head. "Not supposed to."

"Okay." John took the beer and they waved at each other and he started back.

He stopped in the vestibule between cars and stood in the rattling roar of it, looking out the window at the flashing green blur. He put his forehead against the cool glass and hid the blur behind the dark red of his eyelids.

Were there actually a zillion of those guys each going through a slightly different private hell? Something he rarely asked himself was, What would Ernest Hemingway have done in this situation?

He'd probably have the sense to leave it to Milton.

16   The Dangerous
Summer

Castle and Lena met him at the station in Miami, and they drove back to Key West in Castle's old pickup. The drone of the air conditioner held conversation to a minimum, but it kept them cool, at least from the knees down.

John didn't say anything about his encounter with the infinite, or transfinite, not wishing to bring back that fellow with the cane just yet. He did note that the two aspects of his personality hadn't quite become equal partners yet, and small details of this world kept surprising him. There was a monorail being built down to Pigeon Key, where Disney was digging an underwater park. Gasoline stations still sold regular. Castle's car radio picked up TV as well as AM/FM, but sound only.

Lena sat between the two men and rubbed up against John affectionately. That would have been remarkable for John-one and somewhat unusual for John-two. It was a different Lena here, of course, one who had had more of a sex life with John, but there was something more than that, too. She was probably sleeping with Castle, he thought, and the extra attention was a conscious or unconscious compensation, or defense.

Castle seemed a little harder and more serious in this world than the last, not only from his terse moodiness in the pickup, but from recollections of parallel conversations. John wondered how shady he actually was; whether he'd been honest about his police record.

(He hadn't been. In this universe, when Lena had asked him whether he had ever been in trouble with the police, he'd answered a terse no. In fact, he'd done eight hard years in Ohio for an armed robbery he hadn't committed—the real robber hadn't been so stupid, here—and he'd come out of prison bitter, angry, an actual criminal. Figuring the world owed him one, a week after getting out he stopped for a hitchhiker on a lonely country road, pulled a gun, walked him a few yards off the road into a field of high corn, and shot him point-blank at the base of the skull. It didn't look anything like the movies.

(He drove off without touching the body, which a farmer's child found two days later. The victim turned out to be a college student who was on probation for dealing—all he'd really done was buy a kilo of green and make his money back by selling bags to his friends, and one enemy—so the papers said DRUG DEALER FOUND SLAIN IN GANGLAND-STYLE KILLING and the police pursued the matter with no enthusiasm. Castle was in Key West well before the farmer's child smelled the body, anyhow.)

As they rode along, whatever Lena had or hadn't done with Castle was less interesting to John than what *he* was planning to do with her. Half of his self had never experienced sex, as an adult, without the sensory handicaps engendered by scar tissue and severed nerves in the genitals, and he was looking forward to the experience with relish that was obvious, at least to Lena. She encouraged him in not so subtle ways, and by the time they crossed the last bridge into Key West, he was ready to tell Castle to pull over at the first bush.

He left the typewriter in Castle's care and declined help with the luggage. By this time Lena was smiling at his obvious impatience; she was giggling by the time they were momentarily stalled by a truculent door key; laughed her delight as he carried her charging across the room to the couch, then clawing off a minimum of clothing and taking her with fierce haste, wordless, and keeping her on a breathless edge he drifted the rest of the clothes off her and carried her into the bedroom, where they made so much noise Julio banged on the ceiling with a broomstick.

They did quiet down eventually, and lay together in a puddle of mingled sweat, panting, watching the fan push the humid air around. "Guess we both get to sleep in the wet spot," John said.

"No complaints." She raised up on one elbow and traced a figure eight on his chest. "You're full of surprises tonight, Dr. Baird."

"Life is full of surprises."

"You should go away more often—or at least come back more often."

"It's all that Hemingway research. Makes a man out of you."

"You didn't learn this in a book," she said, gently taking his penis and pantomiming a certain motion.

"I did, though; an anthropology book." In another universe. "It's what they do in the Solomon Islands."

"Wisdom of Solomon," she said, lying back. After a pause: "They have anthropology books at JFK?"

"Uh, no." He remembered he didn't own that book in this universe. "Browsing at Wordsworth's."

"Hope you bought the book."

"Didn't have to." He gave her a long slow caress. "Memorized the good parts."

On the other side of town, six days later, she was in about the same position on Castle's bed, and even more exhausted.

"Aren't you overdoing the loving little wifey bit? It's been a week."

She exhaled audibly. "What a week."

"Missed you." He nuzzled her and made an unsubtle preparatory gesture.

"No you don't." She rolled out of bed. "Once is plenty." She went to the mirror and ran a brush through her damp hair. "Besides, it's not me you missed. You missed *it*." She sat at the open window, improving the neighborhood's scenery. "*It's* gonna need a Teflon lining installed."

"Old boy's feelin' his oats?"

"Not feeling *his* anything. God, I don't know what's gotten into him. Four, five times a day; six."

"Screwed, blewed, and tatooed. You asked for it."

"As a matter of fact, I didn't. I haven't had a chance to start my little act. He got off that train with an erection, and he still has it. No woman would be safe around him. Nothing wet and concave would be safe."

"So does that mean it's a good time to bring in Pansy? Or is he so stuck on you he wouldn't even notice her?"

She scowled at the brush, picking hair out of it. "Actually, Castle, I was just about to ask you the same thing. Relying on your well-known expertise in animal behavior."

"Okay." He sat up. "I say we oughta go for it. If he's a walkin' talkin' hard-on like you say . . . Pansy'd pull him like a magnet. You'd have to be a fuckin' monk not to want Pansy."

"Like Rasputin."

"Like who?"

"Never mind." She went back to the brush. "I guess, I guess one problem is that I really am enjoying the attention. I guess I'm not too anxious to hand him over to this champion sexpot."

"Aw, Lena—"

"Really. I do love him in my way, Castle. I don't want to lose him over this scheme."

"You're not gonna lose him. Trust me. You catch him dickin' Pansy, get mad, forgive him. Hell, you'll have him wrapped around your finger."

"I guess. You make the competition sound pretty formidable."

"Don't worry. She's outa there the next day."

"Unless she winds up in love with him. That would be cute."

"He's almost twice her age. Besides, she's a whore. Whores don't fall in love."

"They're women, Castle. Women fall in love."

"Yeah, sure. Just like on TV."

She turned away from him; looked out the window. "You really know how to make a woman feel great, you know?"

"Come on." He crossed over and smoothed her hair. She turned around but didn't look up. "Don't run yourself down, Lena. You're still one hell of a piece of ass."

"Thanks." She smiled into his leer and grabbed him. "If you weren't such a poet I'd trade you in for a vibrator."

---

17 In Praise of His Mistress

Pansy was indeed beautiful, even under normal conditions; delicate features, wasp waist combined with generous secondary sexual characteristics. The conditions under which John first saw her were calculated to maximize sexiness and vulnerability. Red nylon running shorts, tight and very short, and a white sleeveless T-shirt from a local bar that was stamped LAST HETEROSEXUAL IN KEY WEST—all clinging to her golden skin with a healthy sweat, the cloth made translucent enough to reveal no possibility of underwear.

John looked out the screen door and saw her at the other door, struggling with a heavy box while trying to make the key work. "Let me help you," he said through the screen, and stepped across the short landing to hold the box while she got the door open.

"You're too kind." John tried not to stare as he handed the box back. Pansy, of course, was relieved at his riveted attention. It had taken days to set up this operation, and would take more days to bring it to its climax, so to speak, and more days to get back to normal. But she did owe Castle a big favor, and this guy seemed nice enough. Maybe she'd learn something about Hemingway in the process.

"More to come up?" John asked.

"Oh, I couldn't ask you to help. I can manage."

"It's okay. I was just goofing off for the rest of the day."

It turned out to be quite a job, even though there was only one load from a small rented truck. Most of the load was uniform and heavy boxes of books, carefully labeled LIT A–B, GEN REF, ENCY 1–12, and so forth. Most of her furniture, accordingly, was cinder blocks and boards, the standard student bookshelf arrangement.

John found out that despite a couple of dozen boxes marked LIT, Pansy hadn't majored in literature, but rather special education; during the school year, she taught third grade at a school for the retarded in Key Largo. She didn't tell him about the several years she'd spent as a call girl, but if she had, John might have seen a connection that Castle would never have made—that the driving force behind both of the jobs was the same, charity. The more-or-less easy forty dollars an hour for going on a date and then having sex was a factor, too, but she really did like making lonely men feel special, and had herself felt more like a social worker than a woman of easy virtue. And the hundreds of men who had fallen for her, for love or money, weren't responding only to her cheerleader's body. She had a sunny disposition and a natural, artless way of concentrating on a man that made him for a while the only man in the world.

John would not normally be an easy conquest. Twenty years of facing classrooms full of coeds had given him a certain wariness around attractive young women. He also had an impulse toward faithfulness, Lena having suddenly left town, her father ill. But he was still in the grip of the weird overweening horniness that had animated him since inheriting this new body and double-image personality. If Pansy had said "Let's do it," they would be doing it so soon that she would be wise to unwrap the condom before speaking. But she was being as indirect as her nature and mode of dress would allow.

"Do you and your wife always come down here for the summer?"

"We usually go somewhere. Boston's no fun in the heat."

"It must be wonderful in the fall."

And so forth. It felt odd for Pansy, probably the last time she would ever seduce a man for reasons other than personal interest. She wanted it to be perfect. She wanted John to have enough pleasure in her to compensate for the embarrassment of their "accidental" exposure, and whatever hassle his wife would put him through afterward.

She was dying to know why Castle wanted him set up, but he refused to tell. How Castle ever met a quiet, kindly gentleman like John was a mystery, too—she had met some of Castle's friends, and they had other virtues.

Quiet and kindly, but horny. Whenever she contrived, in the course of their working together, to expose a nipple or a little beaver, he would turn around to adjust himself, and blush. More like a teenager, discovering his sexuality, than a middle-aged married man.

He was a pushover, but she didn't want to make it too easy. After they had finished putting the books up on shelves, she said thanks a million; I gotta go now, spending the night housesitting up in Islamorada. You and your wife come over for dinner tomorrow? Oh, then come on over yourself. No, that's all right, I'm a big girl. Roast beef okay? See ya.

Driving away in the rented truck, Pansy didn't feel especially proud of herself. She was amused at John's sexiness, and looking forward to trying it out. But she could read people pretty well, and sensed a core of deep sadness in John. Maybe it was from Vietnam; he hadn't mentioned it, but she knew what the bracelet meant.

Whatever the problem, maybe she'd have time to help him with it—before she had to turn around and add to it.

Maybe it would work out for the best. Maybe the problem was with his wife, and she'd leave, and he could start over . . .

Stop kidding yourself. Just lay the trap, catch him, deliver him. Castle was not the kind of man you want to disappoint.

18 That Was Before I Knew You

J ohn offered to come over to Castle's apartment to look at the typewriter, but he said no, I'll bring it on over, place is a mess. Actually, the place was less messy than it had ever been, what with the woman's touch, but he didn't want to have to go around erasing every trace of Lena's presence just in case John was observant. Lena wasn't wild about the idea of leaving the apartment, either, even for a few hours. They only knew a couple of dozen people in town, but if she ran into one of them, it would be awkward.

She called John every night just after five, to give him a terse report on her father's health. There was little danger of him calling back to Nebraska, but if he did, her mother would cover for her. It wouldn't be the first time.

Castle didn't know how to touch-type, but after several years' working in the prison library, he was pretty good with two fingers. He wrote *All work and no play makes Jack a dull boy* several times. "How about it?"

John pulled the sheet out of the machine and compared it to the Xerox of "Up in Michigan." He grunted, ran the sheet upside down through the platen, and typed the first lines of the story: "Jim Gilmore came to Hortons Bay from Canada. He bought the blacksmith shop from old man Horton. Jim was short and dark with big mustaches and big hands."

He put the Xerox over the typed sheet and held them up to the light. "Hard to say. It's pretty close. But look. The capital *J*'s . . . the capital *H*'s, too; they don't rise far enough off the baseline. You have to bring them up more without displacing the lowercase ones at the same time."

Castle peered at the two pages. "I see what you mean. Well. Back to the drawing board."

"Think it's do-able?"

"Oh yeah. I'm the world's expert on this shit now." He took the top off the typewriter. "The worse that's gonna happen is you or Lena's gonna have to type real slow, do the caps one at a time." He worked the shift lever slowly. "See, I can shim the shift lever to give any amount of upward, what'd you say, displacement." He typed H_HHH_H. "I can plane down and sand wooden shims to fit under the lever, glue a sheet-metal guard on top. One for each letter if I had to. But you don't got to—only five or six of them really goes up."

John nodded, staring at the interior of the machine. "Good, good. You leave it with me. I'll do the photographs and blow them up; then we can fine-tune it."

"You found a place would let you use their stuff?" John had been afraid he'd have to fly up to Boston just to use his darkroom.

"No problem." He laughed. "I stressed the need for absolute privacy, and they said that was the store's ironclad policy. I think a lot of pictures of naked people get developed there." He waved at the Hasselblad standing on a tripod in the corner. "I bought three rolls of super-fine-grain film, Kodak 2415. In between the camera's macro and the enlarger, I could magnify each letter a hundred times, if we needed it."

"Good." Castle put the typewriter's top back on and pressed it gently until it snapped into place. "I'll wait till you have the pictures, then. You give me a call."

"Will do."

As he left, Castle noted the other apartment's door was slightly ajar; Pansy was watching. She probably wondered what the hell was going on.

Funny thing is, Castle thought, maybe we don't have to go through all this bullshit anyhow. Old John is really into it, taking pictures and measuring—no way in hell that's just to set up a handful of reviewers. Deep down inside he's as crooked as the rest of us.

What the hell, though. It's fun to bone Lena. She likes it to hurt.

19 Fiesta

She had baked the roast slowly with wine and fruit juice, along with dried apricots and apples plumped in port wine, seasoned with cinammon and nutmeg and cardamom. Onions and large cubes of acorn squash simmered in the broth. She served new potatoes steamed with parsley and dressed Italian-style, with garlicky olive oil and a splash of vinegar. Small Caesar salad and air-light *pan de agua*, the Cuban bread that made you forget every other kind of bread.

The way to a man's heart, her mother had contended, was through his stomach, and although she was accustomed to aiming rather lower, she thought it was probably a good approach for a long-time married man suddenly forced to fend for himself. That was exactly right for John. He was not much of a cook, but he was an accomplished eater.

He pushed the plate away after three helpings. "God, I'm such a pig. But that was irresistible."

"Thank you." She cleared the table slowly, accepting John's offer to help. "My mother's 'company' recipe. So you think Hadley might have just thrown the stories away, and made up the business about the train?"

"People have raised the possibility. There she was, eight years older than this handsome hubby—with half the women on the Left Bank after him, at least in her mind—and he's starting to get published, starting to build a reputation . . ."

"She was afraid he was going to 'grow away' from her? Or did they have that expression back then?"

"I think she was afraid he would start making money from his writing. She had an inheritance, a trust fund from her grandfather, that paid over two thousand a year. That was plenty to keep the two of them comfortable in Paris. Hemingway talked poor in those days, starving artist, but he lived pretty well."

"He probably resented it, too. Not making the money himself."

"That would be like him. Anyhow, if she chucked the stories to ensure his dependency, it backfired. He was still furious thirty years later—three wives later. He said the stuff had been 'fresh from the mint,' even if the writing wasn't so great, and he was never able to reclaim it."

She opened a cabinet and slid a bottle out of its burlap bag, and selected two small glasses. "Sherry?" He said why not? and they moved into the living room.

The living room was mysteriously devoid of chairs, so they had to sit together on the small couch. "You don't actually think she did it."

"No." John watched her pour the sherry. "From what I've read about her, she doesn't seem at all calculating. Just a sweet gal from St. Louis who fell in love with a cad."

"Cad. Funny old-fashioned word."

John shrugged. "Actually, he wasn't really a cad. I think he sincerely loved every one of his wives . . . at least until he married them."

They both laughed. "Of course it could have been something in between," Pansy said. "I mean, she didn't actually throw away the manuscripts, but she did leave them sitting out, begging to be stolen. Why did she leave the compartment?"

"That's one screwy aspect of it. Hadley herself never said, not on paper. Every biographer seems to come up with a different reason: she went to get a newspaper; she saw some people she recognized and stepped out to talk with them; wanted some exercise before the long trip . . . even Hemingway had two different versions—she went out to get a bottle of Evian water or to buy something to read. That one pissed him off, because she did have an overnight bag full of the best American writing since Mark Twain."

"How would you have felt?"

"Felt?"

"I mean, you say you've written stories, too. What if somebody, your wife, made a mistake and you lost everything?"

He looked thoughtful. "It's not the same. In the first place, it's just a hobby with me. And I don't have that much that hasn't been published—when Hemingway lost it, he lost it for good. I could just go to a university library and make new copies of everything."

"So you haven't written much lately?"

"Not stories. Academic stuff."

"I'd love to read some of your stories."

"And I'd love to have you read them. But I don't have any here. I'll mail you some from Boston."

She nodded, staring at him with a curious intensity. "Oh

hell," she said, and turned her back to him. "Would you help me with this?"

"What?"

"The zipper." She was wearing a clingy white summer dress. "Undo the zipper a little bit."

He slowly unzipped it a few inches. She did it the rest of the way, stood up and hooked her thumbs under the shoulder straps and shrugged. The dress slithered to the floor. She wasn't wearing anything else.

"You're blushing." Actually, he was doing a good imitation of a beached fish. She straddled him, sitting back lightly on his knees, legs wide, and started unbuttoning his shirt.

"Uh," he said.

"I just get impatient. You don't mind?"

"Uh . . . no?"

---

20   On Being Shot Again

J ohn woke up happy but didn't open his eyes for nearly a minute, holding on to the erotic dream of the century. Then he opened one eye and saw it hadn't been a dream: the tousled bed in the strange room, unguents and sex toys on the nightstand, the smell of her hair on the other pillow. A noise from the kitchen; coffee and bacon smells.

He put on pants and went into the living room to pick up the shirt where it had dropped. "Good morning, Pansy."

"Morning, stranger." She was wearing a floppy terry-cloth bathrobe with the sleeves rolled up to her elbows. She turned the bacon carefully with a fork. "Scrambled eggs okay?"

"Marvelous." He sat down at the small table and poured himself a cup of coffee. "I don't know what to say."

She smiled at him. "Don't say anything. It was nice."

"More than nice." He watched her precise motions behind the counter. She broke the eggs one-handed, two at a time, added a splash of water to the bowl, plucked some chives from a window box and chopped them with a small Chinese cleaver, rocking it in a staccato chatter; scraped them into the bowl, and followed them with a couple of grinds of pepper. She set the bacon out on a paper towel, with another towel to cover. Then she stirred the eggs briskly with the fork and set them aside. She picked up the big cast-iron frying pan and poured off a judicious amount of grease. Then she poured the egg mixture into the pan and studied it with alertness.

"Know what I think?" John said.

"Something profound?"

"Huh-uh. I think I'm in a rubber room someplace, hallucinating the whole thing. And I hope they never cure me."

"I think you're a butterfly who's dreaming he's a man. I'm glad I'm in your dream." She slowly stirred and scraped the eggs with a spatula.

"You like older men?"

"One of them." She looked up, serious. "I like men who are considerate . . . and playful." She returned to the scraping. "Last couple of boyfriends I had were all dick and no heart. Kept to myself the last few months."

"Glad to be of service."

"You could rent yourself out as a service." She laughed. "You must have been impossible when you were younger."

"Different." Literally.

She ran hot water into a serving bowl, then returned to her egg stewardship. "I've been thinking."

"Yes?"

"The lost manuscript stuff we were talking about last night, all the different explanations." She divided the egg into four masses and turned each one. "Did you ever read any science fiction?"

"No. Vonnegut."

"The toast." She hurriedly put four pieces of bread in the toaster. "They write about alternate universes. Pretty much like our own, but different in one way or another. Important or trivial."

"What, uh, what silliness."

She laughed and poured the hot water out of the serving bowl, and dried it with a towel. "I guess maybe. But what if . . . what if all of those versions were equally true? In different universes. And for some reason they all came together here." She started to put the eggs into the bowl when there was a knock on the door.

It opened and Ernest Hemingway walked in. Dapper, just twenty, wearing the Italian army cape he'd brought back from the war. He pointed the black-and-white cane at Pansy. "Bingo."

She looked at John and then back at the Hemingway. She dropped the serving bowl; it clattered on the floor without breaking. Her knees buckled and she fainted dead away, executing a half turn as she fell, so that the back of her head struck the wooden floor with a loud thump and the bathrobe drifted open from the waist down.

The Hemingway stared down at her frontal aspect. "Sometimes I wish I were human," it said. "Your pleasures are intense. Simple, but intense." It moved toward her with the cane.

John stood up. "If you kill her—"

"Oh?" It cocked an eyebrow at him. "What will you do?"

John took one step toward it, and it waved the cane. A waist-high brick wall surmounted by needle-sharp spikes appeared between them. It gestured again and an impossible moat appeared, deep enough to reach down well into Julio's living room. It filled with water and a large crocodile surfaced and rested its chin on the parquet floor, staring at John. It yawned teeth.

The Hemingway held up its cane. "The white end. It doesn't kill, remember?" The wall and moat disappeared and the cane touched Pansy lightly below the navel. She twitched minutely but continued to sleep. "She'll have a headache," it said. "And she'll be somewhat confused by the uncommunicable memory of having seen me. But that will all fade, compared to the sudden tragedy of having her new lover die here, just sitting waiting for his breakfast."

"Do you enjoy this?"

"I love my work. It's all I have." It walked toward him, footfalls splashing as it crossed where the moat had been. "You have not personally helped, though. Not at all."

It sat down across from him and poured coffee into a mug that said ON THE SIXTH DAY GOD CREATED MAN—SHE MUST HAVE HAD PMS.

"When you kill me this time, do you think it will 'take'?"

"I don't know. It's never failed before." The toaster made a noise. "Toast?"

"Sure." Two pieces appeared on his plate; two on the Hemingway's. "Usually when you kill people, they stay dead?"

"I don't kill that many people." It spread margarine on its toast, gestured, and marmalade appeared. "But when I do, yeah. They die all up and down the Omniverse, every timespace. All except you." He pointed toast at John's toast. "Go ahead. It's not poison."

"Not my idea of a last meal."

The Hemingway shrugged. "What would you like?"

"Forget it." He buttered the toast and piled marmalade on it, determined out of some odd impulse to act as if nothing unusual were happening. Breakfast with Hemingway, big deal.

He studied the apparition and noticed that it was somewhat translucent, almost like a traditional TV ghost. He could barely see a line that was the back of the chair, bisecting its chest below shoulder-blade level. Was this something new? There hadn't been too much light in the train; maybe he had just failed to notice it before.

"A penny for your thoughts."

He didn't say anything about seeing through it. "Has it occurred to you that maybe you're not *supposed* to kill me? That's why I came back?"

The Hemingway chuckled and admired its nails. "That's a nearly content-free assertion."

"Oh really." He bit into the toast. The marmalade was strong, pleasantly bitter.

"It presupposes a higher authority, unknown to me, that's watching over my behavior and correcting me when I do wrong. Doesn't exist, sorry."

"That's the oldest one in the theologian's book." He set down the toast and kneaded his stomach; shouldn't eat something so strong first thing in the morning. "You can only *assert* the nonexistence of something; you can't prove it."

"What you mean is *you* can't." He held up the cane and looked at it. "The simplest explanation is that there's something wrong with the cane. There's no way I can test it; if I kill the wrong person, there's hell to pay up and down the Omniverse. But what I can do is kill you without the cane. See whether you come back again, some timespace."

Sharp, stabbing pains in his stomach now. "Bastard." Heart pounding slow and hard: shirt rustled in time to its spasms.

"Cyanide in the marmalade. Gives it a certain *frisson*, don't you think?"

He couldn't breathe. His heart pounded once, and stopped. Vicious pain in his left arm, then paralysis. From an inch away, he could just see the weave of the white tablecloth. It turned red and then black.

21   The Sun Also Rises

From blackness to brilliance: the morning sun pouring through the window at a flat angle. He screwed up his face and blinked.

Suddenly smothered in terry cloth, between soft breasts. "John, John."

He put his elbow down to support himself, uncomfortable on the parquet floor, and looked up at Pansy. Her face was wet with tears. He cleared his throat. "What happened?"

"You, you started putting on your foot and . . . you just fell over. I thought . . ."

John looked down over his body, hard ropy muscle and deep tan under white body hair, the puckered bullet wound a little higher on the abdomen. Left leg ended in a stump just above the ankle.

Trying not to faint. His third past flooding back. Walking down a dirt road near Kontum, the sudden loud bang of the mine and he pitched forward, unbelievable pain, rolled over and saw his bloody boot yards away; gray, jagged shinbone sticking through the bloody smoking rag of his pants leg, bright crimson splashing on the dry dust, loud in the shocked silence; another bloodstain spreading between his legs, the deep mortal pain there—and he started to buck and scream and two men held him while the medic took off his belt and made a tourniquet and popped morphine through the cloth and unbuttoned his fly and slowly worked his pants down: penis torn by shrapnel, scrotum ripped open in a bright red flap of skin, bloody gray-blue egg of a testicle separating, rolling out. He fainted, then and now.

And woke up with her lips hard against his, her breath sweet in his lungs, his nostrils pinched painfully tight. He made a strangled noise and clutched her breast.

She cradled his head, panting, smiling through tears, and kissed him lightly on the forehead. "Will you stop fainting now?"

"Yeah. Don't worry." Her lips were trembling. He put a finger on them. "Just a longer night than I'm accustomed to. An overdose of happiness."

The happiest night of his life, maybe of three lives. Like coming back from the dead.

"Should I call a doctor?"

"No. I faint every now and then." Usually at the gym, from pushing too hard. He slipped his hand inside the terry cloth and covered her breast. "It's been . . . do you know how long it's been since I . . . did it? I mean . . . three times in one night?"

"About six hours." She smiled. "And you can say *fuck*. I'm no schoolgirl."

"I'll say." The night had been an escalating progression of intimacies, gymnastics, accessories. "Had to wonder where a sweet girl like you learned all that."

She looked away, lips pursed, thoughtful. With a light fingertip she stroked the length of his penis and smiled when it started to uncurl. "At work."

"What?"

"I was a prostitute. That's where I learned the tricks. Practice makes perfect."

"Prostitute. Wow."

"Are you shocked? Outraged?"

"Just surprised." That was true. He respected the sorority and was grateful to it for having made Vietnam almost tolerable, an hour or so at a time. "But now you've got to do something really mean. I could never love a prostitute with a heart of gold."

"I'll give it some thought." She shifted. "Think you can get up?"

"Sure." She stood and gave him her hand. He touched it

but didn't pull; rose in a smooth practiced motion, then took one hop and sat down at the small table. He started strapping on his foot.

"I've read about those new ones," she said. "The permanent kind."

"Yeah; I've read about them too. Computer interface, graft your nerves onto sensors." He shuddered. "No thanks. No more surgery."

"Not worth it for the convenience?"

"Being able to wiggle my toes, have my foot itch? No. Besides, the VA won't pay for it." That startled John as he said it: here, he hadn't grown up rich. His father had bought a photocopy firm six months before Xerox came on the market. "You say you 'were' a prostitute. Not anymore?"

"No, that was the truth about teaching. Let's start this egg thing over." She picked up the bowl she had dropped when he fainted. It was the same bowl she'd dropped in the other universe. "I gave up whoring about seven years ago."

"As a teenager?"

"Don't be gallant. Partly, I was afraid of AIDS. You make them wear a rubber, but they aren't a hundred percent trustworthy. Then there's premature ejaculation, which I don't normally discuss before breakfast."

"How'd you get into the trade?"

"It was in Iowa City." She laughed. "Sin center of the Midwest. I was minding my own business, making love to a Coke bottle . . ."

"A Coke bottle?"

"The old-fashioned kind, with the narrow neck."

"Thank goodness."

"I was a freshman in college, working my way through school dancing nude in a place called the Sportsman's Lounge. Kind of a cheap joint; I got twenty dollars a set and had to put my own quarters in the jukebox for dancing music." She got the eggs out of the refrigerator.

"Anyhow, Friday and Saturday nights were special. They

had an applause meter, and the girl who got the best reaction won a hundred-dollar bonus. It drove us to extremity."

"I suspect you drove some of the audience to extremity."

"Hope so." She broke the eggs thoughtfully, staring at nothing, remembering. "I'd put this Coke bottle on the stage and dance around it for a couple of numbers. When the time seemed right, I'd squat down and pick it up by the neck. No hands."

"*I'd* applaud."

She stirred the eggs slowly. "I'd play with the bottle awhile, then fake an orgasm and get off the stage." She bit the end off a piece of bacon. "Cold. Why don't I just crumble it up and make an omelet?"

"Sure. So you started taking the customers home?"

"Only in my mind." She smiled. "I'd go home and slip into a nice hot bath and remember their faces. That was the best part of the job. I'd build up all that sexual tension, but I never could let it go, not in front of strangers." She got a small onion out of a bag and sliced off the top and bottom and peeled it carefully.

"One day this guy came up to me between sets and asked whether I'd like to get into an easier line of work."

"He didn't look like a pimp, right?"

"He didn't even look like a *customer*." She concentrated on slicing the onion, tip of her tongue between her teeth. "Coat and tie, mid-forties. I figured he was going to hit on me and got ready to be polite." She put a small piece of the onion in the bacon fat and watched it, turning up the heat a little. "I didn't want to do it with strangers then. Some of the girls went out with customers; they'd make twenty, thirty, maybe fifty dollars at the most. I didn't have children to take care of, or expensive habits, so it wasn't worth it to me." She looked up. "I like to fry the onion first, so it's sweet."

"I'll eat anything you put in front of me."

"Promises, promises. Anyhow, he ran a 'dating service' out on the Coralville Strip that was quite legal, really just a photo album and a Rolodex of phone numbers. We each had a studio portrait and a full-figure shot in an evening gown." She crumbled the bacon into the eggs and washed her hands.

"He'd screen out the obvious goofballs and sleazes; call a few dummy numbers and say no one was available. Everybody else paid twenty bucks and was told where to meet you. He got kickbacks from a couple of restaurants."

"Ever get anybody who thought he was just on a date?"

"Sometimes. Free dinner, maybe a movie—but it could be excruciating. Try two hours at a restaurant with a guy who just stares at you and blushes and can't even say, 'Pass the sugar.' I'd rather put up with a night of kinky sex."

"They get real kinky in Iowa?"

"Huh-uh. I had one guy come in the last Friday of every month who just wanted me to pee on him while he jerked off. Can you imagine? Two hundred bucks to watch someone pee. He even brought his own rubber sheet."

The piece of onion started to sizzle. She scraped the rest of it into the frying pan and stirred it around. The aroma filled the small room; John's stomach growled.

"You got two hundred dollars from everybody?"

"Sometimes more, if I spent the night. Minus twenty bucks to the service."

"So how'd you go from peeing on perverts in Iowa to teaching retarded children in Key Largo?"

"Blind, not retarded."

"Sorry." Wrong universe.

"Three of them are slightly retarded, too, and that's sad. But we have AI machines, artificial intelligence, that do better with them than people do. They have slow Braille interfaces and warm motherly voices that never get upset." She looked up from stirring. "You can't show pity in your voice. They hear tears, they get confused. They think they're hurting you, and then *they* start to cry." She looked back down.

"But they are hurting you."

She shrugged. "There's getting hurt and getting hurt. You got anything against garlic for breakfast?"

"Go for it."

She cocked her head in a quizzical way; they didn't use that phrase here. "Vampire deterrent." She crushed two cloves with the flat of the blade, shucked the skins, minced them, and scraped them into the pan.

"Basically, it was weather. I came down to Lauderdale between semesters, and Jesus, it was so nice. Swimming and rum drinks and sunbathing. Fuck a guy because I like him, or just like the way he looks. That had something to do with it. But it was mainly not slogging around in snow up to your ass until March."

"You found a dating service here?"

"Yeah, here in Key West, escort service." She stirred everything around and poured in the eggs and bacon. "It was a lot different. The guys in Iowa were nice. Even the ones who wanted to tie you up and lick you all over—they were gentlemen before and after. Even during."

"Different down here."

"More transients—I mean, who goes to Iowa City to get laid? But the locals are no pleasure cruise, either.

"In Iowa, the customers were shy single guys who had no luck with women or married men who wanted you to do things their wives wouldn't or couldn't do. Oral or anal sex, or just talk dirty, whatever. Or be young and pretty enough to get their dicks hard." She worked a spatula under the egg expertly and lifted it, tilting the pan slightly. "I had no problem with that, and still don't. Saved more marriages than I hurt."

"Sex therapist."

"In a rough-and-ready way, yeah. Guys want to get their rocks off, maybe with some bells and whistles, then lie there and talk. A lot of them want a listener as much as anything." She repeated the spatula maneuver.

"Down here it's a different story. Tourists, redneck Southerners, Cubans—especially the Mariel Cubans. Pay fifty bucks for a blow job and that gives them the right to slap you around. *Machismo*." She pointed a finger down her throat in a clear gesture. "I saved some money and bailed out."

She divided the omelet in two and slipped each half onto a paper plate and brought them over. "Funny you should say 'retarded'; that's how I started out. Went for my master's in special education at Miami, because of some work I did in Iowa with retarded kids, and adults, too. They're nice people. You treat them halfway decent and they give it back with so much energy. Is it okay?"

"Delicious."

"But on a friend's recommendation, I took a special workshop on teaching the blind. You had to wear a blindfold for two weeks, confined to one floor of a building. Empathy exercise."

"At first it's pretty terrifying. I mean, you wake up in the middle of the night, or is it morning, you can't tell. I had to find the bathroom; at first I couldn't even find my own doorknob. Then I went up and down the hall, couldn't find the push-plate for the john. Nobody else was awake. Finally I had to just squat there in the hall." She took a bite of omelet. "I mean, peeing on a guy who's paying for the privilege is not embarrassing. It's kind of a chuckle. Peeing on the floor because you didn't think to count the steps to the bathroom is mortifying. I stood over it for *hours*, so nobody would step in it, until the janitor came. He said not to worry, it happened all the time. But it was awful. And it taught me a lot about being helpless."

"You couldn't find your way back to your own room?"

"That wasn't the problem. I had a corner room."

"Pansy . . . you know, most people would just let fly and then go back to their room. Nobody would trace it back to them."

She laughed. "You couldn't do *that*."

"How was it after two weeks? Did you get used to being blind?"

"No. A lot of blind people never do. I did develop this sixth sense, though, that everybody has, and some blind people really rely on. You know, walking through a dark room, absolutely dark, you can 'feel' when you're approaching a wall?" He nodded. "It gets hyperdeveloped when you just plain can't see walls.

You can sense them from farther and farther away. You can tell the difference between a wall and a window. It feels like ESP."

"But it's not?"

"They say not. It's a combination of acoustic clues and sensing air pressure on your face and hands. Breasts. But after a while it does feel like a kind of second sight; your imagination supplies the walls and doors and windows—if you've had sight. A person who's never seen, of course, has a universe made up of touch, sound, and smell—" She covered her face with both hands and peeked at him from between the fingers. "God, I'm rattling. Rattling. Sorry."

"Go ahead and rattle. I could listen to you forever."

"No, I'm just . . . just nervous."

"Don't blame you. I gave you quite a scare."

"No. Yes, but . . . aw hell. It's a lot of things."

"Tell me about them. Sometimes therapists need therapy. I owe you about twenty years' worth."

"You don't owe me anything," she said with a sad downward inflection. "Not a damned thing." She studied the egg on her plate, and ate a small piece. "We had an instructor in Miami who was blind since five or six. He was sharp, kind of hard. I liked him. We got it on a couple of times."

"Hard that way too?"

"Like a broomstick. That was part of it." She drew a finger lightly back and forth along her lips. "He couldn't tell if you were pretty or not, of course. That came up because somebody told him I was beautiful. I think every woman was beautiful to him.

"He read your body like a map, like a book. He went over every square inch with his lips, tongue, fingertips. So gentle it was like butterflies all over your body, studying you. Even when he went inside with his finger or tongue, it was like exploration more than stimulation. Of course the result was toe-curling. He kept you wobbling on the edge forever with a nibble here, a lick there—his mouth on erotic places while his fingers were checking out an ankle or the soft place behind your knee. Then when you absolutely couldn't take it any longer—he could tell by the

way you were only touching the bed with your head and heels—
he'd move his tongue down to the business end and make you
come like the turn of the century, come like a jackhammer."

She licked her lips. "But all that time, his dick was just
trailing along like an afterthought. You'd feel it every now and
then, hot and hard and a little wet, but it was as if he was
deliberately ignoring it. Then after you were done, limp as a rag,
he would take the missionary position, slide it in, move a couple
of times, and then give a little shudder. That was it."

John realized he was sweating a little bit. He patted his face
with a napkin. "So the actual orgasm wasn't all that important."

"No. After the fourth or fifth time I asked him, and he said
that in fact, it was sometimes more pain than pleasure. He knew
it was psychological; that because of his physical vulnerability he
couldn't allow himself to lose control. But he also didn't see any
reason to change, since he did love the feel and taste of women,
and could call any of a couple dozen who would be knocking on
his door before he had time to hang up the phone."

John nodded slowly and tapped his artificial foot twice, a
nervous tic he could never prevent once it started. He tapped
twice again and his other foot curled, almost hard enough to
cramp.

"Sounds familiar?"

"Oh yeah. When I came back from Vietnam." He grimaced
and rubbed his face.

"You don't have to talk about it."

"I was like your buddy, you know, Rock of Gibraltar, even
though I couldn't feel much. Too many nerves severed. Nowadays, they could splice them back together, microsurgery. Not in
1968."

"That's . . . that was quite a year."

He smiled. "Year you were born." She nodded. "Once girls
found out how I was hurt, where I was hurt, they opened up for
me. Hate the war and love the soldier. Then when they found
out how long I could last, they hung around. Told their friends."
He laughed. "Jesus, the sixties. Sometimes I had two at a time;

once it was five! We put two mattresses on the floor and they passed me around, called me Dipstick. 'Here, Dipstick.' "

"Still in the sixties?"

"Uh-huh, November twenty-first, 1971—the sixties lasted till 'seventy-four—let's see, room twenty-four of the Holiday Inn in Boston; they were Alice, Toni, Arna, Elizabeth, and Kay. We were drinking Black Velvets—Guinness stout and cheap champagne. Smoking Alice's Acupulco Gold. I remember Alice with her hand on the door, saying 'I'd like you to meet some friends of mine'; turned on the light and there they were, all naked and waiting."

"It's not just books? You really don't forget anything?"

"A blessing and a curse. I even remember things that you can't describe in words. How Elizabeth tasted different from Arna; I can remember that as if I were still in room twenty-four."

She laughed. "I wonder how come your brain doesn't just fill up and stop remembering."

"Yeah." Three slightly different sets of memories—Kay hadn't been there in the first universe; instead, there was a black woman, Willa. In the second universe Alice was wearing a tampon, and Elizabeth, stoned and drunk, kept tugging on the string, ding dong, and then on his penis, dong dong. "Someday it'll freeze up solid, like a log jam. People will ask me why I drink, and I'll say 'to forget,' and it will be the simple sad truth."

"Has anybody ever studied you?"

"Not really. A shrink, twenty-some years ago. I was having trouble with the war, with my wounds. The memory thing came up but he didn't really believe it, and I didn't push it—anyhow, I got EEGs and a positron scan, and no abnormalities showed up. He gave me the sage advice that it would go away eventually, and meanwhile, here's some Valium. Took me a few years to get off that stuff."

She was nodding, thinking furiously. "You know, most people follow a 'learning curve'; like, they sit down in a classroom and they'll remember almost everything the teacher says in the first few minutes—it all gets filed away in long-term memory—

and then they remember less and less as the hour goes on, as the teacher drones on . . ."

"I've seen that curve, yeah. Then they remember again in the last few minutes. Because we're trained to expect the teacher to sum up at the end. But no, I don't do that. Even when I'm bored, I remember everything. I could reel back, verbatim, dull lectures I heard in my freshman year—and tell you who was sitting around me on that day, what they were wearing, and so forth."

"Wow."

"But it's not like real knowledge; it's not *there* the way American literature is, or any of my hobbies, like photography or classical music. It's almost like an endless library of trivial videotapes. I concentrate a certain way and that day-hour-minute comes back. It isn't integrated into a vast body of knowledge, which is why I don't rule the world. Or the English department, for that matter."

"One day is about the same as the other? I mean, you remember yesterday as strongly as last week or ten years ago?"

"Yesterday . . . last night." He reached over and squeezed her hand. "That will stay strong, nearer to the surface. Times of intense pleasure or pain always do. Sometimes I can cover up a bad memory with a good one, if I catch it quickly enough. You'll help me a lot with that."

"God, I hope so."

"I know you will. Nothing like you has ever happened to me before." Except in two other universes.

"The war is still close to the surface, too?"

"Some of it. The woundings, I can play back chapter and verse. Slow motion. Macro close-up." He shuddered and his foot tapped twice; twice again. A blank look came into his eyes and with a ragged exhalation he squeezed her hand hard enough to make her wince.

She covered his clenched hand with her other one and waited until his eyes came back to the present. "I can't do this to you."

"You . . . can't do what?"

"Oh, lie. Keep lying." She stood up abruptly and went to the refrigerator. "Want a beer?"

"Lying? No, no thanks. What lying?"

She opened a beer, still not looking at him. "I like you, John. I really like you. But I didn't just . . . spontaneously fall into your arms." She took a healthy swig and started pouring some from the bottle into a glass.

"I don't understand."

She walked back, concentrating on pouring the beer, then sat down gracelessly. She took a deep breath and let it out, staring at his chest. "Castle put me up to it."

"*Castle?*"

She nodded. "Sylvester Castlemaine, boy wonder."

John set back stunned. "But you said you don't do that anymore," he said without too much logic. "Do it for money."

"Not for money," she said in a flat, hurt voice.

"I should've known. A woman like you wouldn't want . . ." he made a gesture that dismissed his body from the waist down.

"You do all right. Don't feel sorry for yourself." Her face showed a pinch of regret for that, but she plowed on. "If it were just the obligation, once would have been enough. I wouldn't've had to fuck and suck all night long to win you over."

"No," he said. "That's true. Just the first moment, when you undressed. That was enough."

"I owe Castle a big favor. A friend of mine was going to be prosecuted for involving a minor in prostitution. It was a setup, pure and simple."

"She worked for the same outfit you did?"

"Yeah, but this was free-lance. I think it was the escort service that set her up, sort of delivered her and the man in return for this or that."

She sipped at the beer. "Guy wanted a three-way. My friend had met this girl a couple of days before at the bar where she worked part-time . . . she looked old enough; said she was in the biz."

"She was neither?"

"God knows. Maybe she got caught as a juvie and made a deal. Anyhow, he'd just slipped it to her and suddenly cops comin' in the windows. Threw the book at him. 'Two inches, twenty years,' my friend said. He was a county commissioner somewhere, with enemies. Almost dragged my friend down with him. I'm *sorry*." Her voice was angry.

"Don't be," John said, almost a whisper. "It's understandable. Whatever happens, I've got last night."

She nodded. "So two of the cops who were going to testify got busted for possession, cocaine. The word came down, and everybody remembered the woman was somebody else."

"So what did Castle want you to do? With me?"

"Oh, whatever comes natural—or *un*natural, if that's what you wanted. And later be doing it at a certain time and place, where we'd be caught in the act."

"By Castle?"

"And his trusty little video camera. Then I guess he'd threaten to show it to your wife, or the university."

"I wonder. Lena . . . I've had other women."

"But not lately."

"No. Not for years."

"It might be different now. She might be starting to feel, well, insecure."

"Any woman who looked at you would feel insecure."

She shrugged. "That could be part of it. Could it cost you your job, too?"

"I don't see how. It would be awkward, but it's not as if you were one of my students—and even that happens, without costing the guy his job." He laughed. "Poor old Larry. He had a student kiss and tell, and had to run the speakers' committee for four or five years. Got allergic to wine and cheese. But he made tenure."

"So what is it?" She leaned forward. "Are you an addict or something?"

"Addict?"

"I mean how come you even *know* Castle? He didn't pick

your name out of a phone book and have me come seduce you, just to see what would happen."

"No, of course not."

"So? I confess, you confess."

John passed a hand over his face and pressed the other hand against his knee, bearing down to keep the foot from tapping. "You don't want to be involved."

"What do you call last night, Spin the Bottle? I'm *involved!*"

"Not the way I mean. It's illegal."

"Oh golly. Not really."

"Let me think." John picked up their dishes and limped back to the sink. He set them down there and fiddled with the straps and pad that connected the foot to his stump, then poured himself a cup of coffee and came back, not limping.

He sat down slowly and blew across the coffee. "What it is, is that *Castle* thinks there's a scam going on. He's wrong. I've taken steps to ensure that it couldn't work." His foot tapped twice as he realized that wasn't true, not here: in this universe he hadn't enlisted Abramson's unconscious collaboration by presenting the what-if-I-did-this-as-an-elaborate-joke hypothesis. He'd meant to, but the department head had been on vacation when John went up to work in JFK. "Couldn't work."

"You think. You hope."

"No. I'm sure. Anyhow, I'm stringing Castle along because I need his expertise in a certain matter."

" 'A certain matter,' yeah. Sounds wholesome."

"Actually, that part's not illegal."

"So tell me about it."

"Nope. Still might backfire."

She snorted. "You know what might *back*fire. Fucking with Castle."

"I can take care of him."

"You don't know. He may be more dangerous than you think he is."

"He talks a lot."

"You men." She took a drink and poured the rest of the beer

into the glass. "Look, I was at a party with him couple of years ago. He was drunk, got into a little coke, started babbling."

"In vino veritas?"

"Yeah, and Coke is It. But he said he'd killed three people, strangers, just to see what it felt like. He liked it. I more than halfway believe him."

John looked at her silently for a moment, sorting out his new memories of Castle. "Well . . . he's got a mean streak. I don't know about murder. Certainly not over this thing."

"Which is?"

"You'll have to trust me. It's not because of Castle that I can't tell you." He remembered her one universe ago, lying helpless while the Hemingway lowered its cane onto her nakedness. "Trust me?"

She studied the top of the glass, running her finger around it. "Suppose I do. Then what?"

"Business as usual. You didn't tell me anything. Deliver me to Castle and his video camera; I'll try to put on a good show."

"And when he confronts you with it?"

"Depends on what he wants. He knows I don't have much money." John shrugged. "If it's unreasonable, he can go ahead and show the tape to Lena. She can live with it."

"And your department head?"

"He'd give me a medal."

22 in our time

So it wasn't the cane. He ate enough cyanide to kill a horse, but evidently only in one universe.

You checked the next day in all the others?

All 119. He's still dead in the one where I killed him on the train—

That's encouraging.

—but there's no causal resonance in the others.

Oh, but there is some resonance. He remembered you in the universe where you poisoned him. Maybe in all of them.

That's impossible.

Once is impossible. Twice is a trend. A hundred and twenty means something is going on that we don't understand.

What I suggest—

No. You can't go back and kill them all one by one.

If the wand had worked the first time, they'd all be dead anyhow. There's no reason to think we'd cause more of an eddy by doing them one at a time.

It's not something to experiment with. As you well know.

I don't know how we're going to solve it otherwise.

Simple. Don't kill him. Talk to him again. He may be getting frightened, if he remembers both times he died.

Here's an idea. What if someone else killed him?

I don't know. If you just hired someone—made him a direct agent of your will—it wouldn't be any different from the cyanide. Maybe as a last resort. Talk to him again first.

All right. I'll try.

23 Education of the Flesh

"Just the first couple of lines," Castle said. "I'll take it over for him to do the blowups."

"Okay." Lena had the wooden blocks laid out in alphabetical order to the right of the typewriter. "Jim Gilmore came to Hortons Bay from Canada," she typed, very slowly. About every fourth letter, she had to position a wooden shim underneath the key before striking it. "He bought the blacksmith shop from old man Hortom." Wrong key. "Shit."

"Do it over."

"This is enough."

"You gotta get good at it. Do it over."

"All right, all right." She put in a new piece of paper and typed with deliberate exaggerated care. Castle paced.

She rolled the paper out of the platen and set it down silently. "I don't know."

Castle looked at it. "Looks okay to me."

"That's not what I mean. I don't know whether we ought to do it."

"After all this shit? You on the rag, or what?"

"I don't mean the project in general." She waved a hand weakly in the direction of the window. "I mean blackmailing John. I don't want to do it to him anymore. I'm not sure why I wanted to in the first place. I don't think—"

Castle clamped a hand around her upper arm and pulled her up out of the swivel chair. "Lee . . . na. He's *boning* her."

"Even as we speak," she said, returning his level stare. "But it's not his fault."

He shoved her back down into the chair. "Jesus. *Women!*" He stomped to the window and leaned, framing his overmuscled body in the light.

"Just listen to me for—" He came back in three huge steps and stabbed his finger at her face.

"No, *you* listen to *me*. I set the date. I got the video camera. I got the whole fuckin' thing set up. I mean lights camera action—and we are by God gonna *do* it!"

"But—"

"Pansy's outa town for two days startin' tomorrow. Way he's been, she comes back, he's gonna jump her bones like a goddamn werewolf. I'll be in the bedroom closet with the quiet little Sony."

"But we don't *have* to!" She was almost shouting. "He's obviously had a change of heart. He's put so much into it, it's for real now. He'll do it anyhow."

Castle stared, silent, body clenched. She paused, tried to get the pleading out of her voice. "You go ahead and take the pictures. But don't confront him then and there."

"Sure. Spend the whole fuckin' night in the closet."

"That's not . . . you can have the woman get him out of there. Have them go to dinner or something—but don't hurt him with the pictures. Not unless we have to. Let me talk to him first."

He folded his arms and glowered at her. "He'll do better work as a willing partner," she said. "You can't hold a gun to someone's head and say 'Write a novel.' "

"Little late to be changin' everything."

"Not all that much is changed. We just don't hurt John."

"*You're* the one that's got the fuckin' change a heart. Thought you wanted to nail the bastard."

"Not my heart that's changed. My mind. I'm thinking straighter now. We have to work as a team."

Castle returned to the window and stared down at the sun-baked street. "Maybe you're right. Maybe." He didn't want to let go of the image he'd savored for weeks, waiting until just the right moment and kicking the door open—surprise! But it would be smarter to hold on to the tapes—hell, John Baird might be famous in a couple of years, rich and famous. That would be the time to bring out the videotape.

He turned and sat on the sill. Lena looked small and helpless, standing in the shadows with her arms crossed over her chest. He savored the feeling of control. "Tell you what. We'll make a deal."

"What kind of a deal?"

"I don't hurt your husband. We take the pictures but keep it secret. They're just insurance. But in return . . . you don't stop with me."

"I—I hadn't planned to. We'll just have to be more careful." She gave a nervous short laugh. "Besides, even if John found out, he couldn't very well play the outraged faithful husband."

"That's right. And we'll have proof." He stared at her for a second, then crossed quickly over and slipped the typed sheet into a blue plastic folder. "Be back in an hour or so. You be ready."

"Sure." He nodded and walked out the door with a slight swagger.

"Ready," she whispered. She stepped into the bathroom and in the strong light inspected her shoulder. Red marks from his fingers, maybe not bad enough to cause bruises. She started the bath water running and went into the kitchen for a cup of coffee and a magazine.

She set the coffee on the edge of the tub and undressed in two motions. With one foot on the toilet seat, she used a hand mirror to check for damage from the morning session. A little swelling. She liked what Castle did with his battering ram, but once or twice a week would be plenty. She looked forward to getting back to John and his more gentle, clever, ways.

She dabbed on a little cortisone cream and then slipped into the warm water. Soak for a while, then a cool shower, then more cream, then go dutifully lie on the bed with your legs apart, waiting, or maybe on the couch with your ass waving in the breeze. Or maybe it's not too late to become a nun.

---

24 Of Wounds and Other Causes

Although John found it difficult to concentrate, trying not to think about Pansy, this was the best time he would have for the forseeable future to summon the Hemingway demon and try to do something about exorcising it. He didn't want either of the women around if the damned thing went on a killing spree again. They might just do as he did, and slip over into another reality—as unpleasant as that was, it was at least living—but the Hemingway had said otherwise. There was no reason to suspect it was not the truth.

Probably the best way to get the thing's attention was to resume work on the Hemingway pastiche. He decided to rewrite the first page to warm up, typing it out in Hemingway's style:

ALONG WITH YOUTH

1. Mitraigliatrice

The dirt on the side of the trench was never dry in the morning . If Fever could find a dry newspaper he could put it between his chest and the dirt when he went out to lean on the side of the trench and wait for the light .First light was the best time . You might have luck and see a muzzle flash to aim at . But patience was better than luck . Wait to see a helmet or a head without a helmet .

Fever looked at the enemy trench line through a rectangular box of wood that pushed through the trench wall at about ground level . The other end of the box was covered with a square of gauze the color of dirt . A man looking directly at it might see the muzzle flash when Fever fired through the box . But with luck , the flash would be the last thing he saw .

Fever had fired through the gauze six times . He'd potted at least three Austrians . Now the gauze had a ragged hole in the center . One bullet had come in the other way , an accident , and chiseled a deep gouge in the floor of the wooden box .Fever knew that he would be able to see the splinters sticking up before he could see any detail at the enemy trench line.

That would be maybe twenty minutes . Fever wanted a cigarette . There was plenty of time to go down in the bunker

and light one . But it would fox his night vision . Better to
wait .

Fever heard movement before he heard the voice . He
picked up one of the grenades on the plank shelf to his left
and his thumb felt the ring on the cotter pin . Someone was
crawling in front of his position . Slow crawling but not too
quiet . He slid his left forefinger through the ring and
waited .

————Help me, came a strained whisper .

Fever felt his shoulders tense . Of course many
Austrians could speak Italian .

————I am wounded . Help me . I can go no farther .

————What is your name and unit , Fever whispered through
the box .

————Jean-Franco Dante . Four forty-seventh.

That was the unit that had taken such a beating at the
evening show . ————At first light they will kill me .

————All right. But I 'm coming over with a grenade
in my hand . If you kill me , you die as well .

————I will commend this logic to your superior
officer . Please hurry .

Fever slid his rifle into the wooden box and eased
himself to the top of the trench . He took the grenade out of
his pocket and carefully worked the pin out, the arming lever
held secure . He kept the pin around his finger so he could
replace it .

He inched his way down the slope , guided by the man's whispers . After a few minutes his probing hand found the man's shoulder . -----Thank God . Make haste , now .

The soldier's feet were both shattered by a mine . He would have to be carried .

-----Don't cry out, Fever said . This will hurt .

-----No sound , the soldier said . And when Fever raised him up onto his back there was only a breath . But his canteen was loose . It fell on a rock and made a loud hollow sound .

Firecracker pop above them and the night was all glare and bobbing shadow . A big machine-gun opened up rong, cararong, rong , rong . Fever headed for the parapet above as fast as he could but knew it was hopeless . He saw dirt spray twice to his right and then felt the thud of the bullet into the Italian , who said " Jesus " as if only annoyed , and they almost made it then but on the lip of the trench a hard snowball hit Fever behind the kneecap and they both went down in a tumble . They fell two yards to safety but the Italian was already dead .

Fever had sprained his wrist and hurt his nose fall- ing and they hurt worse than the bullet . But he couldn't move his toes and he knew that must be bad . Then it started to hurt .

A rifleman closed the Italian's eyes and with the help of another clumsy one dragged Fever down the trench to the medical bunker . It hurt awfully and his shoe filled up with

blood and he puked . They stopped to watch him puke and then
dragged him the rest of the way .

   The surgeon placed him between two kerosene lanterns .
He removed the puttee and shoe and cut the bloody pants leg with
a straight razor . He rolled Fever onto his stomach and had four
men hold him down while he probed for the bullet . The pain was
great but Fever was insulted enough by the four men not to cry
out . He heard the bullet clink into a metal dish . It sounded
like the canteen .

"That's a little too pat, don't you think?" John turned
around and there was the Hemingway, reading over his shoulder.
" 'It sounded like the canteen,' indeed." Khaki army uniform
covered with mud and splattered with bright blood. Blood
dripped and pooled at its feet.

"So shoot me. Or whatever it's going to be this time. Maybe
I'll rewrite the line in the next universe."

"You're going to run out soon. You only exist in eight more
universes."

"Sure. And you've never lied to me." John turned back
around and stared at the typewriter, tensed.

The Hemingway sighed. "Suppose we talk, instead."

"I'm listening."

The Hemingway walked past him toward the kitchen, leaving a spatter trail. "Want a beer?"

"Not while I'm working."

"Suit yourself." It limped into the kitchen, out of sight, and
John heard it open the refrigerator and pry the top off of a beer.
It came back out as the five-year-old Hemingway, dressed up in
girl's clothing, both hands clutching an incongruous beer bottle.
It set the bottle on the end table and crawled up onto the couch
with childish clumsiness.

"Where's the cane?"

"I knew it wouldn't be necessary this time," it piped. "It occurs to me that there are better ways to deal with a man like you."

"Do tell." John smiled. "What is 'a man like me'? One on whom your cane for some reason doesn't work?"

"Actually, what I was thinking of was curiosity. That is supposedly what motivates scholars. You *are* a real scholar, not just a rich man seeking legitimacy?"

John looked away from the ancient eyes in the child face. "I've sometimes wondered myself. Why don't you cut to the chase, as we used to say. A few universes ago."

"I've done spot checks on your life through various realities," the child said. "You're always a Hemingway buff, though you don't always do it for a living."

"What else do I do?"

"It's probably not healthy for you to know. But all of you are drawn to the missing manuscripts at about this time, the seventy-fifth anniversary."

"I wonder why that would be."

The Hemingway waved the beer bottle in a disarmingly mature gesture. "The Omniverse is full of threads of coincidence like that. They have causal meaning in a dimension you can't deal with."

"Try me."

"In a way, that's what I want to propose. You will drop this dangerous project at once, and never resume it. In return, I will take you back in time, back to the Gare de Lyon on December fourteenth, 1921."

"Where I will see what happens to the manuscripts."

Another shrug. "I will put you on Hadley's train, sufficiently before she said the manuscripts were stolen. You will be able to observe for an hour or so, without being seen. As you know, some people have theorized that there never was a thief; never was an overnight bag; that Hadley simply threw the writings away. If that's the case, you won't see anything dramatic. But the absence of the overnight bag would be powerful indirect proof."

John looked skeptical. "You've never gone to check it out for yourself?"

"If I had, I wouldn't be able to take you back. I can't exist twice in the same timespace, of course."

"How foolish of me. Of course."

"Is it a deal?"

John studied the apparition. The couch's plaid upholstery showed through its arms and legs. It did appear to become less substantial each time. "I don't know. Let me think about it for a couple of days."

The child pulled on the beer bottle and it stretched into a long amber stick. It turned into the black-and-white cane. "We haven't tried cancer yet. That might be the one that works." It slipped off the couch and sidled toward John. "It does take longer and it hurts. It hurts 'awfully.'"

John got out of the chair. "You come near me with that and I'll drop-kick you into next Tuesday."

The child shimmered and grew and became Hemingway in his mid-forties, a big-gutted barroom brawler. "Sure you will, champ." It held out the cane so that the tip was inches from John's chest. "See you around." It disappeared with a barely audible pop, and a slight breeze as air moved to fill its space.

John thought about that as he went to make a fresh cup of coffee. He wished he knew more about science. The thing obviously takes up space, since its disappearance caused a vacuum, but there was no denying that it was fading away.

Well, not fading. Just becoming more transparent. That might not affect its abilities. A glass door is as much of a door as an opaque one, if you try to walk through it.

He sat down on the couch, away from the manuscript so he could think without distraction. On the face of it, this offer by the Hemingway was an admission of defeat. An admission, at least, that it couldn't solve its problems by killing John over and over. That was comforting. He would just as soon not die again, except for the one time.

But maybe he should. That was a chilling thought. If he

made the Hemingway kill him another dozen times, another hundred . . . what kind of strange creature would he become? A hundred overlapping autobiographies, all perfectly remembered? Surely the brain has a finite capacity for storing information; he'd "fill up," as Pansy had said. Or maybe it wasn't finite, at least in his case—but that was logically absurd. There are only so many cells in a brain. Of course he might be "wired" in some way to the John Bairds in all the other universes he had inhabited.

And what would happen if he died in some natural way, not dispatched by an interdimensional assassin? Would he still slide into another identity? That was a lovely prospect: sooner or later, he would be 130 years old, on his deathbed, dying every fraction of a second for the rest of eternity.

Or maybe the Hemingway wasn't lying, this time, and he had only eight lives left. In context, the possibility was reassuring.

The phone rang; for a change, John was grateful for the interruption. It was Lena, saying her father had come home from the hospital, much better, and she thought she could come on home day after tomorrow. Fine, John said, feeling a little wicked; I'll borrow a car and pick you up at the airport. Don't bother, Lena said; besides, she didn't have a flight number yet.

John didn't press it. If, as he assumed, Lena was in on the plot with Castle, she was probably here in Key West, or somewhere nearby. If she had to buy a ticket to and from Omaha to keep up her end of the ruse, the money would come out of John's pocket.

He hung up and, on impulse, dialed her parents' number. Her father answered. Putting on his professorial tone, he said he was Maxwell Perkins, Blue Cross claims adjuster, and he needed to know the exact date when Mr. Monaghan entered the hospital for this recent confinement. He said you must have the wrong guy; I haven't been inside a hospital in twenty years, knock on wood. Am I not speaking to John Franklin Monaghan? No, this is John *Frederick* Monaghan. Terribly sorry, natural mistake. That's okay; hope the other guy's okay, goodbye, good night, sir.

So tomorrow was going to be the big day with Pansy. To his knowledge, John hadn't been watched during sex for more than twenty years, and never by a disinterested, or at least dispassionate, observer. He hoped that knowing they were being spied upon wouldn't affect his performance. Or knowing that it would be the last time.

A profound helpless sadness settled over him. He knew that the last thing you should do, in a mood like this, was go out and get drunk. It was barely noon, anyhow. He took enough money out of his wallet for five martinis, hid the wallet under a couch cushion, and headed for Duval Street.

25   Shootism vs. Sport

Lena was lying in bed, enjoying the breeze from the oscillating fan playing over her skin, still damp from the shower. She heard the screen door slap. Castle called "C'mere, Lena," and she slid obediently off the bed.

She stepped into the living room and her hands suddenly fluttered to cover her nakedness. There was a blond woman with Castle who started and blushed and covered her own clothed breasts in reflex sympathy. Lena turned her back on Castle's horselaugh and tried to walk with dignity back into the bedroom. While she was putting on her halter and shorts she heard the woman say, "You can be a real shit sometimes, Castle, you know that?"

When she returned, the blonde's face was dark red, perhaps from anger as well as embarrassment. "I'm sorry, Mrs. Baird," she said.

"You two girls have something in common."

"Do tell. Hello, Pansy."

"He said you were in Miami."

"So I lied. I like surprises."

"I'm *sorry*." Her voice trembled, and she looked as if she were about to cry.

"Don't be." Lena took a step toward Pansy, who backed away uncertainly, and then joined her in an embrace. She stared over the woman's shoulder at Castle. "Sylvester just enjoys other people's pain."

"I told you not to call me that."

The shorter woman's tears were wet against her neck. She squeezed her own eyes shut. "Thylvesther, Thylvesther," she lisped. "I t'ot I taw a puddy tat."

"Bitch." He tore her away from the other woman and slapped her open-handed on the cheek so hard it knocked her to the floor. He towered over her and punctuated his speech with a stabbing finger: "You *never*! Call me *that*! *Again*!"

"Jesus, Castle—"

He spun to glare at Pansy. "That's what the faggots in prison used to call me. I don't have to put up with it!"

Lena felt her side teeth gingerly. When she withdrew her finger from her mouth, it trailed a catenary thread of bloody saliva. She slumped, looking at the floor. "When I asked you whether you ever were in trouble with the law, you said no."

"Yeah. Must've lied again."

"Last time you'll lie to me," Lena said.

"Yeah, sure." She stood up slowly. "Where you goin'?"

"Bathroom. Do you *mind*? I want to count my teeth."

"If I wanted to break your fuckin' teeth I woulda broke your fuckin' teeth."

The bathroom mirror confirmed that the blood was just

from a cut on the inside of her cheek. There might be a nice bruise to match the one on her arm.

How did she let herself get into this? He was wild and exciting at first, with a kind of raffish charm. Over the past couple of weeks the charm had evaporated, though, as the brutality increased. This is what he really is: a sadistic abuser of women.

She had found his gun last week, hidden in the corner of the closet behind a stack of boxes. She pulled it out now, a double-barreled twelve-gauge shotgun with barrels only a foot and a half long, the stock sawed off and sanded down to a pistol grip. A real sportsman's weapon.

She stood in the doorway and leveled it at his back. He was arguing with Pansy. "Oh, Castle," she said. "Sylvester."

He spun around and froze when he saw the gun.

"I think I should do the world a favor," she said. "Get out of the way, Pansy."

A squint of concentration creased his face. Then he slowly relaxed. His voice was calm. "You're not going to do it."

"You've been wrong about me before." The weapon trembled in Lena's hands but she kept it trained on his chest.

He shrugged and walked toward her, not fast, not slow. Standing right in front of her, he said, "Here," softly, and with one finger raised both barrels up to his head. He leaned forward so that his forehead was resting on them.

"You have to cock it first." He reached forward and pushed back both external hammers. "Now you just pull the triggers, and we have a nice new ceiling decoration."

For a few seconds nobody breathed. His eyes were closed and he had a relaxed smile. She stared at him, unbelieving, and glanced over at Pansy, who was crowded into a far corner, chewing on a knuckle.

He slowly, gently, took the gun from her. Almost in a whisper, he said, "You don't have the balls for it, Lena. It takes balls to kill a man." He reversed the weapon and slid both barrels between her breasts. With a toothy, almost friendly, smile, he pulled both triggers. The hammers slapped down on empty chambers with a loud double click.

"Lucky for us you didn't load it."

"You would've killed me."

"Only if you'd loaded it, sweetheart. Fair's fair."

Pansy sat down on the floor with a loud thump, half fainting. "I don't believe you, Castle." In the opposite corner an invisible man smiled and silently applauded.

26 Dying, Well or Badly

John had just about decided it was too early in the day to get drunk. He had polished off two martinis in Sloppy Joe's and then wandered uptown because the tourists were getting to him and a band was setting up, depressingly young and cheerful. Heavy metal rock. Hemingway would've kicked in their speakers.

He found a grubby bar he'd never noticed before, dark and smoky and hot. In the other universes it was a yuppie boutique. Three Social Security drunks were arguing politics almost loudly enough to drown out the game show on the television. The whole package seemed to go well with the headache and sour stomach he'd reaped from the martinis and the walk in the sun. He got a beer and some peanuts and a couple of aspirin from the bartender, and sat in the farthest booth with a copy of the local classified-ad newspaper. Somebody had obscurely carved FUCK ANARCHY into the tabletop.

Nobody else in this world knows what anarchy *is*, John

thought, and the helpless anomie came back, intensified somewhat by drunken sentimentality. What he would give to go back to the first universe and undo this all by just not . . .

Would that be possible? The Hemingway was willing to take him back to 1921; why not back a few weeks? Where the hell was that son of a bitch when you needed him, it, whatever.

The Hemingway appeared in the booth opposite him, an Oak Park teenager smoking a cigarette. "I felt a kind of vibration from you. Ready to make your decision?"

"Can the people at the bar see you?"

"No. And don't worry about appearing to be talking to yourself. A lot of that goes on around here."

"Look. Why can't you simply take me back to a couple of weeks before we met on the train, back in that first universe? I'll just . . ." The Hemingway was shaking its head slowly. "You can't."

"No. As I explained, you already exist there—"

"You said that *you* couldn't be in the same place twice. How do you know I can't?"

"How do you know you can't swallow that piano? You just can't."

"You thought I couldn't talk about you, either; you thought your stick would kill me. I'm not like normal people."

"That's certainly true. But this is something more, well, more basic to reality than the cane."

"What the hell does 'basic to reality' mean? Something is real or it isn't."

"That's a queer pronouncement for someone in your situation."

John ate a peanut thoughtfully. "Try this on for size. At eleven forty-six on June third, a man named Sylvester Castlemaine sat down in Dos Hermosas and started talking with me about the lost manuscripts. The forgery would never have occurred to me if I hadn't talked to him. Why don't you go back and keep him from going into that café? Or just go back to eleven-thirty and kill him."

The Hemingway smiled maliciously. "You don't like him much."

"It's more fear than like or dislike." He rubbed his face hard, remembering. "Funny how things shift around. He actually was kind of likable the first time I met him. Then you killed me on the train, and in the subsequent universe he became colder, more serious. Then you killed me in Pansy's apartment, and in this universe he has turned mean. Dangerously mean, like a couple of men I knew in Vietnam. The ones who really love the killing. Like you, evidently."

It blew a chain of smoke rings before answering. "I don't 'love' killing, or anything else. I have a complex function and I fulfill it, because that is what I do. That sounds circular because of the limitations of human language.

"I can't go killing people right and left just to see what happens. When a person dies at the wrong time it takes forever to clean things up. Not that it wouldn't be worth it in your case. But I can tell you with certainty that killing Castlemaine would not affect the final outcome."

"How can you say that? He's responsible for the whole thing." John finished off most of his beer, and the Hemingway touched the mug and it refilled. "Not poison?"

"Wouldn't work," it said morosely. "I'd gladly kill Castlemaine any way you want—cancer of the penis is a suggestion—if there was even a fighting chance that it would clear things up. The reason I know it wouldn't is that I am not in the least attracted to that meeting. There's no probability nexus associated with it, the way there was with your buying the Corona or starting the story on the train, or writing it down here. You may think that you would never have come up with the idea for the forgery on your own, but you're wrong."

"That's preposterous."

"Nope. There are universes in this bundle where Castle isn't involved. You may find that hard to believe, but your beliefs aren't important."

John nodded noncommittally and got his faraway remembering look. "You know . . . reviewing in my mind all the conversations we've had, all five of them, the only substantive reason you've given me not to write this pastiche, and I quote, is that 'I or someone like me will have to kill you.' Since that doesn't seem to be possible, why don't we try some other line of attack."

It put out the cigarette by squeezing it between thumb and forefinger. There was a smell of burning flesh. "All right, try this: give it up or I'll kill Pansy. Then Lena."

"I've thought of that, and I'm gambling that you won't, or can't. You had a perfect opportunity a few days ago—maximum dramatic effect—and you didn't do it. Now you say it's an awfully complicated matter."

"You're willing to gamble with the lives of the people you love?"

"I'm gambling with a lot. Including them." He leaned forward. "Take me into the future instead of the past. Show me what will happen if I succeed with the Hemingway hoax. If I agree that it's terrible, I'll give it all up and become a plumber."

The old, wise Hemingway shook a shaggy head at him. "You're asking me to please fix it so you can swallow a piano. I can't. Even I can't go straight to the future and look around; I'm pretty much tied to your present and past until this matter is cleared up."

"One of the first things you said to me was that you were from the future. And the past. And 'other temporalities,' whatever the hell that means. You were lying then?"

"Not really." It sighed. "Let me force the analogy. Look at the piano."

John twisted half around. "Okay."

"You can't eat it—but after a fashion, I can." The piano suddenly transformed itself into a piano-shaped mountain of cold capsules, which immediately collapsed and rolled all over the floor. "Each capsule contains a pinch of sawdust or powdered ivory or metal; the whole piano in about a hundred thousand capsules. If I take one with each meal, I will indeed eat the piano, over the course of the next hundred-some years. That's not a long time for me."

"That doesn't prove anything."

"It's not a *proof*; it's a demonstration." It reached down and picked up a capsule that was rolling by, and popped it into its mouth. "One down, ninety-nine thousand nine hundred ninety-nine to go. So how many ways could I eat this piano?"

"Ways?"

"I mean I could have swallowed any of the hundred thousand first. Next I can choose any of the remaining ninety-nine thousand nine hundred ninety-nine. How many ways can—"

"That's easy. One hundred thousand factorial. A huge number."

"Go to the head of the class. It's ten to the godzillionth power. That represents the number of possible paths—the number of futures—leading to this one guaranteed, preordained event: my eating the piano. They are all different, but in terms of whether the piano gets eaten, their differences are trivial.

"On a larger scale, every possible trivial action that you or anybody else in this universe takes puts us into a slightly different future than would have otherwise existed. An overwhelming majority of actions, even seemingly significant ones, make no difference in the long run. All of the futures bend back to one central, unifying event—except for the ones that you're screwing up!"

"So what is this big event?"

"It's impossible for you to know. It's not important, anyhow." Actually, it would take a rather cosmic viewpoint to consider the event unimportant: the end of the world.

Or at least the end of life on Earth. Right now there were two middle-aged politicians who on 11 August 2006 would be president and premier of their countries. On that day, one would insult the other beyond forgiveness, and a button would be pushed, and then another button, and by the time the sun set on Moscow, or rose on Washington, there would be nothing left alive on the planet at all—from the bottom of the ocean to the top of the atmosphere; not a cockroach, not a paramecium, not a virus, and all because there are some things a man just doesn't have to take, not if he's a real man.

Hemingway wasn't the only writer who felt that way, but he was the one with the most influence on this generation. The apparition who wanted John dead or at least not typing didn't know exactly what effect his pastiche was going to have on Hemingway's influence, but it was going to be decisive and ultimately negative. It would prevent or at least delay the end of the world in a whole bunch of universes, which would put a zillion adjacent realities out of kilter, and there would be hell to pay all up and down the Omniverse. Many more people than the six billion here would die—and it's even possible that all of Reality would unravel, and collapse back to the Primordial Hiccup from whence it came.

"If it's not important, then why are you so hell-bent on keeping me from preventing it? I don't believe you."

"*Don't* believe me, then!" At an imperious gesture, all the capsules rolled back into the corner and reassembled into a piano, with a huge crashing chord. None of the barflies heard it. "I should think you'd cooperate with me just to prevent the unpleasantness of dying over and over."

John had the expression of a poker player whose opponent has inadvertently exposed his hole card. "You get used to it," he said. "And it occurs to me that sooner or later I'll wind up in a universe that I really like. This one doesn't have a hell of a lot to recommend it." His foot tapped twice and then twice again.

"No," the Hemingway said. "It will get worse each time."

"You can't know that. This has never happened before."

"True so far, isn't it?"

John considered it for a moment. "Some ways. Some ways not."

The Hemingway shrugged and stood up. "Well. Think about my offer." The cane appeared. "Happy cancer." It tapped him on the chest and disappeared.

The first sensation was utter tiredness, immobility. When

he strained to move, pain slithered through his muscles and viscera, and stayed. He could hardly breathe, partly because his lungs weren't working and partly because there was something in the way. In the mirror beside the booth he looked down his throat and saw a large white mass, veined, pulsing. He sank back into the cushion and waited. He remembered the young wounded Hemingway writing to his parents from the hospital with ghastly cheerfulness: "If I should have died it would have been very easy for me. Quite the easiest thing I ever did." I don't know, Ernie; maybe it gets harder with practice. He felt something tear open inside and hot stinging fluid trickled through his abdominal cavity. He wiped his face and a patch of necrotic skin came off with a terrible smell. His clothes tightened as his body swelled.

"Hey, buddy, you okay?" The bartender came around in front of him and jumped. "Christ, Harry, punch nine-one-one!"

John gave a slight ineffectual wave. "No rush," he croaked.

The bartender cast his eyes to the ceiling. "Always on my shift?"

27 The Denunciation

"Assault and battery," Lena said. "Assault with a deadly weapon."

The big sergeant nodded tiredly and tapped out two numbers, one-fingered, on the keyboard. "Okay, and you were living with him?"

"Staying with him."

"He's not your boyfriend?"

"He's neither. Neither a boy nor a friend. If you mean 'Did you have sex with him?' the answer is yes."

"Willingly."

"Willingly. Frequently. With gay abandon, or heterosexual abandon. Is it relevant to the assault charge?"

He turned slowly in the squeaky chair and put both elbows on the table that separated him from the two women. He folded his arms and looked at the table for a moment, and then looked at Pansy, and then looked at Lena. "Couple of ways. Your relationship with him determines whether it goes to the Domestic Violence unit."

"That would be ludicrous," Lena said.

"Nothing domestic about that creep," Pansy added.

He nodded but shrugged. "Before you file formal charges, you ought to talk to a counselor, either in our Domestic Violence unit or downtown at the Battered Spouse Protection Group."

"First I want that bastard behind bars."

"Maybe you do and maybe you don't." He rummaged around in a drawer and came up with a card for the battered spouse group. "We can pick him up and hold him for twenty-four hours. Then it's his word against yours; his lawyer against yours."

"I have an eyewitness."

He looked at Pansy and swung the monitor around so she could see her record. "Prostitution. Public nuisance."

"Both suspended," she said. "I did public service."

"Yeah. And you were a defense witness for the child-prostitution trial of one Jennifer Oldenberg. So was Sylvester Castlemaine. There's a confidential note by his name, and yours, that makes me think your testimony wouldn't be worth a lot in this matter."

"Is this *bruise* worth something?" Lena said. "The cut inside my mouth?"

He just looked at her. "Last month a woman came in here with an earlobe bitten off, blood everywhere, bruises from head to toe, two broken ribs. Hysterical. We went out to pick up her boyfriend. It took three big men and a can of Mace, and one of the cops got a broken nose and lost a tooth.

"Next morning the lady comes down and visits this guy in the holding cell. They get all lovey and she drops charges and demands that we release him—'course, we got him on assaulting an officer, so he'll be away for a while. But still."

"It's not relevant. I'm no flighty bimbo. He didn't chew off my earlobe but he did put a sawed-off shotgun up to my chest and pull both triggers."

That actually caused him to raise an eyebrow. "Sawed-off shotgun?"

"Unloaded, of course."

"We might could bring him in on that. If the barrels're under eighteen inches long." He pushed a button. "ADW, anyhow. Did you know the gun wasn't loaded?"

"No."

A scratchy speaker on the desk said, "Dispatch."

"You got a black-and-white down there right now?"

"Martinez and Stanley typin' up reports."

"Send Martinez up." He looked at Lena. "Did he?"

"Did he what?"

"Know the gun wasn't loaded."

"I don't think so. I think he meant to kill me." She grimaced. "I'm not sure, actually. Maybe he could tell it wasn't loaded by the weight or balance of it. Maybe he just meant to *scare* me to death."

"Well. Maybe we can scare him some. Give him a nice mean cellmate overnight." He smiled. "A little gay abandon. But he'll probably be out tomorrow."

"Even if the shotgun's illegal?"

"Did you see those four bail bondsman's offices across the street when you came in? If he has a car or a TV set, he can be out in a couple of days, at least temporarily."

"That's all you can do?" Pansy said.

"No. We can and will put a restraining order on him, essentially saying that if he lays a finger on you, he's in deep trouble."

"Make it both of us," Lena said.

"Okay, but I gotta be honest with you. Restraining order's only as good as the guy it's on. All it really means is that if he slaps you around again, we can haul him in for a hearing where he has to explain why we shouldn't hold him in contempt of court."

"That'll scare the hell out of him," Pansy said.

"I don't make the laws." He tapped the table in front of Lena. "You don't live here."

"Most summers. The rest of the time we're in Boston."

"The best thing I could give you would be a plane ticket to Boston. Tonight. You oughta pack up and be outa here before he's back on the street."

"It's not that simple."

"So what can I tell ya?" A Hispanic in a patrolman's uniform came up to the stairs, and the detective crooked a finger at him. "This is Sergeant Martinez. You gonna pick up her boyfriend on a six-one-one—" Martinez looked at Lena's face and nodded gravely. "But you want to treat it like ADW. He's got a sawed-off shotgun."

"Jesus."

"Yeah. So check out a weapons group just in case. We'll get a search warrant to look for the shotgun, but I want him off the street right *now*."

"I'll get Stanley."

"Okay. Ladies, you go downstairs with the sergeant, give him the information he wants. Then find a place to stay and call me with the phone number."

"Maybe this battered spouse bunch?" Pansy said.

"No. Let's go home." Pansy looked at her. "Have to face John sooner or later. I'd appreciate it if you came with me."

She giggled. "Hey. Why not?"

"I want to see the look on his face when we walk in together." She scribbled the number down on a pad and handed it to the detective. "Pansy's my husband's girlfriend. He doesn't know I know."

"Right," the detective said slowly, and watched the two women walk to the stairway with Martinez. Then he studied the phone number, as if its digits might contain a clue to the mysteries of female human behavior.

The clerk next to him laughed. "Five'll get you ten she comes back with the other eye black."

"No bet." He typed the number out on his console; the address automatically appeared underneath. "I'm a lover, not a gambler." He looked back at the empty stairwell and pantomimed a kiss.

The other man laughed. "Yeah."

28   Death in the Afternoon

John woke up behind a Dumpster in an alley. It was high noon and the smell of fermenting garbage was revolting. He didn't feel too well in any case; as if he'd drunk far too much and passed out behind a Dumpster, which was exactly what had happened in this universe.

In this universe. He stood slowly to a quiet chorus of creaks and pops, brushed himself off, and staggered away from the malefic odor. Staggered, but not limping—he had both feet again, in this present. There was a hand-sized numb spot at the top of his left leg where a .51 caliber machine-gun bullet had missed his balls by an inch and ended his career as a soldier.

And started it as a writer. He got to the sidewalk and stopped dead. This was the first universe where he wasn't a college professor. He taught occasionally—sometimes creative writing; sometimes Hemingway—but it was only a hobby now, and a nod toward respectability.

He rubbed his fringe of salt-and-pepper beard. It covered the bullet scar there on his chin. He ran his tongue along the metal teeth the army had installed thirty years ago. Jesus. Maybe it does get worse every time. Which was worse, losing a foot or getting your dick sprayed with shrapnel, numb from severed nerves, plus bullets in leg and face and arm? If you knew there was a Pansy in your future, you would probably trade a foot for a whole dick. Though she had done wonders with what was left.

Remembering furiously, not watching where he was going, he let his feet guide him back to the oldsters' bar where the Hemingway had showed him how to swallow a piano. He pushed through the door and the shock of air-conditioning brought him back to the present.

Ferns. Perfume. Lacy underthings. An epicene salesclerk sashayed toward him, managing to look worried and determined at the same time. His nose was pierced, decorated with a single diamond button. "Si-i-ir," he said in a surprisingly deep voice. "May I *help* you?"

Crotchless panties. Marital aids. The bar had become a store called the French Connection. "Guess I took a wrong turn. Sorry." He started to back out.

The clerk smiled. "Don't be shy. Everybody needs *some*-thing here."

The heat was almost pleasant in its heavy familiarity. John stopped at a convenience store for a six-pack of greenies and walked back home.

An interesting universe; much more of a divergence than the other had been. Reagan had survived the Hinckley assassination somehow, and actually went on to a second term. Bush was elected, rather than succeeding to the presidency, and the country had not gone to war in Nicaragua. The Iran-contra scandal nipped it in the bud.

The United States was actually cooperating with the Soviet Union in a flight to Mars. There were no De Sotos. Could there be a connection?

And in this universe he had actually met Ernest Hemingway.

Havana, 1952. John was eight years old. His father, a doctor in this universe, had taken a break from the New England winter to treat his family to a week in the tropics. John got a nice sunburn the first day, playing on the beach while his parents tried the casinos. The next day they made him stay indoors, which meant tagging along with his parents, looking at things that didn't fascinate eight-year-olds.

For lunch they went to La Florida, on the off chance that they might meet the famous Ernest Hemingway, who supposedly held court there when he was in Havana.

To John it was a huge dark cavern of a place, full of adult smells. Cigar smoke, rum, beer, stale urine. But Hemingway was indeed there, at the end of the long dark wood bar, laughing heartily with a table full of Cubans. Basques, actually; jai alai players, though that made a difference to neither John nor his parents.

John was vaguely aware that his mother resembled some movie actress, but he couldn't have guessed that that would change his life. Hemingway glimpsed her and then stood up and was suddenly silent, mouth open. Then he laughed and waved a huge arm. "Come on over here, daughter."

The three of them rather timidly approached the table, John acutely aware of the careful inspection his mother was receiving from the silent Cubans. "Take a look, Mary," Hemingway said to the small blond woman knitting at the table. "The Kraut."

The woman nodded, smiling, and agreed that John's mother looked just like Marlene Dietrich ten years before. Hemingway invited them to sit down and have a drink, and they accepted with an air of genuine astonishment. He gravely shook John's hand, and spoke to him as he would to an adult. Then he shouted to the bartender in fast Spanish, and in a couple of minutes his parents had huge daiquiris and he had a Coke with a wedge of lime in it, tropical and grown-up. The waiter also brought a tray of boiled shrimp. Hemingway even ate the heads and tails, crunching loudly, which John thought was much more impressive than any Nobel Prize. Hemingway might have agreed, since he hadn't yet received one, and Faulkner had.

For more than an hour, two Cokes, John watched as his parents sat hypnotized in the aura of Hemingway's famous charm. He put them at ease with jokes and stories and questions—for the rest of his life, John's father would relate how impressed he was with the sophistication of Hemingway's queries about cardiac medicine—but it was obvious even to a child that they were in awe, electrified by the man's presence.

Later that night, John's father asked him what he thought of Mr. Hemingway. Forty-four years later, John of course remembered his exact reply: "He has fun all the time. I never saw a grown-up who plays so hard."

Interesting. That meeting was where his eidetic memory started. He could remember a couple of days before it pretty well, because they had still been close to the surface. In other universes, he could remember back well before grade school. It gave him a strange feeling. All of the universes were different, but this was the first one where the differentness was so tightly connected to Hemingway.

He was flabby in this universe, fat over old tired muscle, like Hemingway at his age, perhaps, and he felt a curious anxiety that he suddenly realized was a real *need* to have a drink. Not just desire, not just thirst. If he didn't have a drink, something very very bad would happen. He knew that was irrational. Knowing didn't help.

John carefully mounted the stairs up to their apartment, stepping over the fifth one, also rotted in this universe. He put the beer in the refrigerator and took from the freezer a bottle of icy vodka—that was different—and poured himself a double shot and knocked it back, medicine drinking.

That would spike the hangover pretty well. He pried the top

off a beer and carried it into the living room, thoughtful as the alcoholic glow radiated through his body. He sat down at the typewriter and picked up his air pistol, a fancy Belgian target model. He cocked it and with a practiced two-handed grip aimed at a paper target across the room. The pellet struck less than half an inch low.

All around the room, the walls were pocked from where he'd fired at roaches and, once, a scorpion. Very Hemingwayish, he thought; in fact, most of the ways he was different from the earlier incarnations of himself were in Hemingway's direction.

He spun a piece of paper into the typewriter and made a list:

```
                EH & me --

-- both had doctor fathers

-- both forced into music lessons

-- in high school wrote derivative stuff that didn't show promise

-- Our war wounds were evidently similar in severity and
location.  Maybe my groin one was worse; army doctor there
said that in Korea (and presumably WII), without helicopter
dustoff, I would have been dead on the battlefield.  (Having
been wounded in the kneecap and foot myself, I know that H's
story about carrying the wounded guy on his back is unlikely.
It was a month before I could put any stress on the knee.) He
mentioned genital wounds, possibly similar to mine, in a letter
to Bernard Baruch, but there's nothing in the Red Cross report
about them.

    But in both cases, being wounded and surviving was the
central experience of our youth.  Touching death.

-- We each wrote the first draft of our first novel in six weeks
(but his was better and more ambitious).

-- Both had unusual critical success from the beginning.

-- Both shy as youngsters and gregarious as adults.

-- Always loved fishing and hiking and guns; I loved the bullfight
from my first corrida, but may have been influenced by H's books.

-- Spain in general
```

—have better women than we deserve

— drink too much

— hypochondria

— accident proneness

— a tendency toward morbidity

— One difference. I will never stick a shotgun in my mouth and pull the trigger. Leaves too much of a mess.

He looked up at the sound of the cane tapping. The Hemingway was in the Karsh wise-old-man mode, but was nearly transparent in the bright light that streamed from the open door. "What do I have to do to get your attention?" it said. "Give you cancer again?"

"That was pretty unpleasant."

"Maybe it will be the last." It half sat on the arm of the couch and spun the cane around twice. "Today is a big day. Are we going to Paris?"

"What do you mean?"

"Something big happens today. In every universe where you're alive, this day glows with importance. I assume that means you've decided to go along with me. Stop writing this thing in exchange for the truth about the manuscripts."

As a matter of fact, he had been thinking just that. Life was confusing enough already, torn between his erotic love for Pansy and the more domestic, but still deep, feeling for Lena . . . writing the pastiche was kind of fun, but he did have his own fish to fry. Besides, he'd come to truly dislike Castle, even before Pansy had told him about the setup. It would be fun to disappoint him.

"You're right. Let's go."

"First destroy the novel." In this universe, he'd completed seventy pages of the Up-in-Michigan novel.

"Sure." John picked up the stack of paper and threw it into the tiny fireplace. He lit it in several places with a long barbecue match, and watched a month of work go up in smoke. It was only a symbolic gesture, anyhow; he could retype the thing from memory if he wanted to.

"So what do I do? Click my heels together three times and say 'There's no place like the Gare de Lyon'?"

"Just come closer."

John took three steps toward the Hemingway and suddenly fell up down sideways—

He knew dying; this was worse than dying. He was torn apart and scattered throughout space and time, being nowhere and everywhere, everywhen, being a screaming vacuum forever—

Grit crunched underfoot and coal smoke was choking thick in the air. It was cold. Gray Paris skies glowered through the long skylights, through the complicated geometry of the black steel trusses that held up the high roof. Bustling crowds chattering French. A woman walked through John from behind. He pressed himself with his hands and felt real.

"They can't see us," the Hemingway said. "Not unless I will it."

"That was awful."

"I hoped you would hate it. Now you know how I spend most of my timespace. Come on." They walked past vendors selling paper packets of roasted chestnuts, bottles of wine, stacks of baguettes and cheeses. There were strange resonances as John remembered the various times he'd been here more than a half century in the future. It hadn't changed much.

"There she is." The Hemingway pointed. Hadley looked worn, tired, dowdy. She stumbled, trying to keep up with the porter who strode along with her two bags. John recalled that she was just recovering from a bad case of the grippe. She'd probably still be home in bed if Hemingway hadn't sent the telegram urging her to come to Lausanne because the skiing was so good, at Chamby.

"Are there universes where Hadley doesn't lose the manuscripts?"

"Plenty of them," the Hemingway said. "In some of them he doesn't sell 'My Old Man' next year, or anything else, and he throws all the stories away himself. He gives up fiction and becomes a staff writer for the *Toronto Star*. Until the Spanish Civil War; then he joins the Abraham Lincoln Battalion, sometimes Brigade, and is killed driving an ambulance. His only affect on American literature is one paragraph in *The Autobiography of Alice B. Toklas*."

"But in some, the stories actually do see print?"

"Sure, including the novel, which is usually called *Along with Youth*. There." Hadley was mounting the steps up into a passenger car. There was a microsecond of agonizing emptiness, and they materialized in the passageway in front of Hadley's compartment. She and the porter walked through them.

"Merci," she said, and handed the man a few sous. He made a face behind her back.

"*Along with Youth*?" John said. The same title he had used.

"It's a pretty good book, sort of prefiguring *A Farewell to Arms*, but he does a lot better in universes where it's not published. *The Sun Also Rises* gets more attention then."

Hadley stowed both the suitcase and the overnight bag under the seat. Then she frowned slightly, checked her wristwatch, and left the compartment, closing the door behind her. She looked back to verify that her luggage wasn't visible from the passageway.

"Interesting," the Hemingway said. "So she didn't leave it out in plain sight, begging to be stolen."

"Makes you wonder," John said. "This novel, *Along with Youth*. Was it about World War One?"

"The trenches in Italy," the Hemingway said. "What difference does that make?"

A young man stepped out of the shadows of the vestibule, looking in the direction Hadley had gone. Then he turned around and faced the two travelers from the future.

It was Ernest Hemingway. He smiled. "Close your mouth, John. You'll catch flies." He opened the door to the compartment, picked up the overnight bag, and carried it into the next car.

John recovered enough to chase after him. He had disappeared.

The Hemingway followed, translating instantly. "What *is* this?" John said. "I thought you couldn't be in two timespaces at once."

"That wasn't me."

"It sure as hell wasn't the real Hemingway. He's in Lausanne with Lincoln Steffens."

"Maybe he is and maybe he isn't."

"He knew my *name!*"

"That he did." The Hemingway was getting fainter as John watched.

"Was he another one of you? Another STAB agent?"

"No. Not possible." It peered at John. "What's happening to you?" Its features went slack with a look of disbelief. "Oh no. It was *you.*"

"What was me?"

"Just now." It gestured toward the other car. "The bag, the manuscripts. Of *course!*"

John laughed. "Sure. Just call me Papa. I'm a dead ringer for the guy."

The Hemingway was a vague ghost. The cane appeared in its hand, and it stabbed at John over and over, but to no effect. "Doesn't work anymore," John said.

Hadley burst into the car and ran right through them, shouting in French for the conductor. She was carrying a bottle of Evian water.

"Well," John said, "that's what—"

The Hemingway was gone. John just had time to think *Marooned in 1922?* when the railroad car and the Gare de Lyon dissolved in an inbursting cascade of black sparks and it was no easier to handle the second time, spread impossibly thin across all those light-years and millenniums, wondering whether it was going to last forever this time, realizing that it did anyhow, and coalescing with an impossibly painful *snap:*

Looking at the list in the typewriter. He reached for the

Heineken; it was still cold. He set it back down. "God," he whispered. "I hope that's that."

The situation called for higher octane. He went to the freezer and took out the vodka. He sipped the gelid syrup straight from the bottle, and almost dropped it when out of the corner of his eye he saw the overnight bag.

He set the open bottle on the counter and sleepwalked over to the dining room table. It was the same bag, slightly beat up, monogrammed EHR, Elizabeth Hadley Richardson. He opened it and inside was a thick stack of manila envelopes.

He took the top one and carried it and the vodka bottle back to his chair. His hands were shaking. He opened the folder and stared at the familiar typing.

ERNEST M. HEMINGWAY

ONE - EYE FOR MINE

────*It*────

ᵀever stood up . In the moon light he could ₓₓ see blood starting on his hands . His pants were torn at the knee and he knew it would be bleeding ~~there~~ too . He watched the lights of the caboose disappear in the trees where the track curved .

That lousy crut of a brakeman . He would get him ~~xxxxxxx~~ some day .
                        scuffed
Fever ~~xxxxxxx~~ off the end of a tie and sat down to pick the cinders out of his hands and knee . He could use some water . The brakeman had his canteen .

He could smell a campfire . He wondered if it would be smart ₜo go find it . He knew about the wolves ., the human kind that lived along the rails and the disgusting things they liked

He wasn't afraid of them but you didn't look for trouble.

You don't have to look for trouble, his father would

say. Trouble will find you. His father didn't tell him about

wolves, though, ~~or about women~~.

There was a noise in the brush. Pever stood up and

slipped his hand around the horn grip of the fat Buck clasp

knife in his pocket.

The screen door creaked open, and he looked up to see
Pansy walk in with a strange expression on her face. Lena followed, looking even stranger. Her left eye was swollen shut and
most of that side of her face was bruised blue and brown. There
was a butterfly bandage over a cut on her forehead.

He stood up, shaking with the sudden clash of emotions.
"What—"

"Castle," Pansy said. "He got outa hand."

"I'll call the police."

"We've already been there," Lena said, her voice distorted.
"It's all over."

"Of course. We can't work with—"

"No, I mean he's a criminal. He's wanted in Mississippi for
second-degree murder. They went to arrest him, hold him for
extradition. So no more Hemingway hoax."

"What Hemingway?" Pansy said. "Hoax?"

"We'll tell you all about it," Lena said, and pointed at the
bottle. "A little early, don't you think? You could at least get us
a couple of glasses." John stood up, obviously stunned. He looked
at Lena, then Pansy, then Lena. She rolled her eyes. "I know
that you know that she knows that he knows. Whatever. I'm

sorry for the whole mess. I love you. I think she does too. Okay? A couple of glasses?"

John went into the kitchen, almost floating with vodka buzz and anxious confusion. "What do you want with it?" Pansy said oh-jay and Lena said ice. Then Lena screamed.

He turned around and there was Castle standing in the doorway, grinning. He had a revolver in his right hand and the sawed-off shotgun in his left.

"You cunts," he said. "You fuckin' cunts. Go to the fuckin' cops."

There was a butcher knife in the drawer next to the refrigerator, but he didn't think Castle would stand idly by and let him rummage for it. Nothing else that might serve as a weapon, except the air pistol. Castle would know that it couldn't do much damage.

He looked at John. "You three're gonna be my hostages. We're gettin' outa here, lose 'em up in the Everglades. They'll have a make on my pickup, though."

"We don't have a car," John said.

"I *know* that, asshole! There's a Hertz right down on One. You go rent one and don't try nothin' cute. I so much as *smell* a cop, I blow these two cunts away."

He turned back to the women and grinned crookedly, talking hard-guy through his teeth. "Like I did those two they sent, the spic and the nigger. They said somethin' about comin' back with a warrant to look for the shotgun and I was just bein' as nice as could be, I said hell, come on in, don't need no warrant. I got nothin' to hide, and when they come in I take the pistol from the nigger and blow the spic's brains out and shoot the nigger in the balls. You shoulda heard him. Some nigger. Took four more rounds to shut him up."

Wonder if that means the pistol is empty, John thought. He had Pansy's orange juice in his hand. It was an old-fashioned Smith & Wesson .357 Magnum six-shot, but from this angle he couldn't tell whether it had been reloaded. He could try to blind Castle with the orange juice.

He stepped toward him. "What kind of car do you want?"

"Just a *car*, damnit. Big enough." A siren whooped about a block away. Castle looked wary. "Bitch. You told 'em where you'd be."

"No," Lena pleaded. "We didn't tell them anything."

"Don't do anything stupid," John said.

Two more sirens, closer. "I'll show you *stupid!*" He raised the pistol toward Lena. John dashed the orange juice in his face.

It wasn't really like slow motion. It was just that John didn't miss any of it. Castle growled and swung around and in the cylinder's chambers John saw five copper-jacketed slugs. He reached for the gun and the first shot shattered his hand, blowing off two fingers, and struck the right side of his chest. The explosion was deafening and the shock of the bullet was like being hit simultaneously in the hand and chest with baseball bats. He rocked, still on his feet, and coughed blood spatter on Castle's face. He fired again, and the second slug hammered him on the other side of the chest, this time spinning him half around. Was somebody screaming? Hemingway said it felt like an icy snowball, and that was pretty close, except for the inside part, your body saying Well, time to close up shop. There was a terrible familiar radiating pain in the center of his chest, a sharper pain than the two bullets, and John realized that he was having a totally superfluous heart attack. He pushed off from the dinette and staggered toward Castle again. He made a grab for the shotgun and Castle emptied both barrels into his abdomen. It sounded like doors slamming. Mary said it sounded like two drawers slamming, when Hemingway in Idaho in the downstairs hall put both barrels in his mouth and pulled the triggers. How the hell did he pull the second trigger, John had always wondered, with his brains all blown out. He dropped to his knees and then fell over on his side. He couldn't feel anything. Things started to turn dim and red. Was this going to be the last time?

Castle cracked the shotgun and the two spent shells flew up in an arc over his shoulder. He took two more out of his shirt pocket and dropped one. When he bent over to pick it up, Pansy leaped past him. In a swift motion that was almost graceful—it came to John that he had probably practiced it over and over, acting out fantasies—he slipped both shells into their chambers and closed the gun with a flip of the wrist. The screen door was stuck. Pansy was straining at the knob with both hands. Castle put the muzzles up to the base of her skull and pulled one trigger. Most of the fragmenting pieces of her head covered the screen or went through the small hole the blast made. The crown of her skull, a bloody bowl, bounced off two walls and went spinning into the kitchen, long beautiful blond hair fanning out behind it. Her body did a spastic little dance and folded, streaming life.

Lena was suddenly on his back, clawing at his face. He spun and slammed her against the wall. She wilted like a rag doll and he hit her hard with the pistol on the way down. She unrolled at his feet, vomiting into her hands, and with his mouth wide open laughing silently he lowered the shotgun and blasted her point-blank in the crotch. Her body jackknifed and John tried with all his will not to die but blackness crowded in and the last thing he saw was that evil grin as Castle reloaded again, peering out the window, presumably at the police.

It wasn't the terrible sense of being spread infinitesimally thin over an infinity of pain and darkness; things had just gone black, like closing your eyes. If this is death, John thought, there's not much to it.

But it changed. There was a little bit of pale light, some vague figures, and then colors bled into the scene; and after a moment of disorientation he realized he was still in the apartment, but apparently floating up by the ceiling. Lena was conscious, barely, twitching, staring stunned at the river of blood that pumped from between her legs. Pansy looked unreal, headless but untouched from the neck down, lying in a relaxed, improbable posture like a knocked-over department-store dummy, blood still spurting from a neck artery out through the screen door.

His own body was a mess, the abdomen completely excavated by buckshot. Inside the huge wound, behind the torn coils of intestine, the shreds of fat and gristle, the blood, the shit, he could see sharp splintered knuckles of backbone. Maybe it hadn't hurt so much because the spinal cord had been severed in the blast.

He had time to be a little shocked at himself for not feeling more. Of course most of the people he'd known who had died did die this way, in loud spatters of blood and brains. Even after thirty years of the occasional polite heart attack or stroke carrying off friend or relative, most of the many dead people he knew had died in the jungle, in Technicolor.

He had been a hero there, in this universe. That would have surprised his sergeants in the original one. Congressional Medal of Honor, so-called, which hadn't hurt the sales of his first book. Knocked out the NVA machine-gun emplacement with their own satchel charge, then hauled the machine gun around and wiped out their mortar and command squads. He managed it all with bullet wounds in the face and triceps. Of course without the bullet wounds he wouldn't have lost his cool and charged the machine gun in the first place, but that wasn't noted in the citation.

A pity there was no way to trade the medals in, melt them down into one big fat bullet and use it to waste that crazy motherfucker who was ignoring the three people he'd just killed, laughing like a hyena while he shouts obscenities at the police gathering down below. John had killed more people than that, but out of horrible necessity, and he had done a lifetime of penance with typewriter and checkbook.

Castle wasn't human. It would be a grave disservice to a whole order of creatures to even call him an animal.

Castle fires a shot through the lower window and then ducks and a spray of automatic-weapons fire shatters the upper window, filling the air with a spray of glass; bullets and glass fly painlessly through John where he's floating and he hears them spatter into the ceiling and suddenly everything is white with plaster dust—it starts to clear and he is much closer to his body, drawing down closer and closer; he merges with it and there's an instant of blackness and he's looking out through human eyes again:

A dull noise and he looked up to see hundreds of shards of glass leap up from the floor and fly to the window; plaster dust in billows sucked up into bullet holes in the ceiling, which then disappeared.

The top windowpane re-formed as Castle *un*crouched, pointed the shotgun, then jerked forward as a blossom of yellow flame and white smoke rolled back into the barrel.

His hand was whole, the fingers restored. He looked down and saw rivulets of blood running back into the hole in his abdomen, then individual drops; then it closed and the clothing restored itself; then one of the holes in his chest closed up and then the other.

The clothing was unfamiliar. A tweed jacket in this weather? His hands had turned old, liver spots forming as he watched. Slow like a plant growing, slow like the moon turning, thinking slowly too, he reached up and felt the beard and could see out of the corner of his eye that it was white and long. He was too fat, and a belt buckle bit painfully into his belly. He sucked in and pried out and looked at the buckle, yes, it was old brass and said GOTT MIT UNS, the buckle he'd taken from a dead German so long ago. The buckle Hemingway had taken.

John got to one knee. He watched fascinated as the stream of blood gushed back into Lena's womb, disappearing as Castle, grinning, stabbed the barrels in between her legs, flinched, and did a complicated dance in reverse (while Pansy's decapitated body writhed around and jerked upright); Lena, sliding up off the floor, leaped up between the man's back and the wall, then fell off and ran backward as he flipped the shotgun up to the back of Pansy's neck and seeming gallons of blood and tissue came flying from every direction to assemble themselves into the lovely head and face, distorted in terror as she jerked awkwardly at the door and then ran backward, past Castle as he did a graceful pirouette, unloading the gun and placing one shell on the floor, which flipped up to his pocket as he stood and put the other one there.

John stood up and walked through some thick resistance toward Castle. Was it *time* resisting him? Everything else was still moving in reverse: Two empty shotgun shells sailed across the room to snick into the weapon's chambers; Castle snapped it shut and wheeled to face John—

But John wasn't where he was supposed to be, or who; Castle just had time to look puzzled. As the shotgun swung around, John grabbed the barrels—hot!—and pulled the pistol out of Castle's waistband. He lost his grip on the shotgun barrels just as he jammed the pistol against Castle's heart and fired. A spray of blood from all over the other side of the room converged on Castle's back and John felt the recoil sting of the Magnum just as the shotgun muzzle cracked hard against his teeth, mouthful of searing heat then blackness forever, back in the featureless infinite timespace hell that the Hemingway had taken him to, forever, but in the next instant, a new kind of twitch, a twist . . .

28   The Time Exchanged

What does that mean, you "lost" him?

We were in the railroad car in the Gare de Lyon, in the normal observation mode. This entity that looked like Hemingway walked up, greeted us, took the manuscripts, and disappeared.

Just like that.

No. He went into the next car. John Baird ran after him. Maybe that was my mistake. I translated instead of running.

That's when you lost him.

Both of them. Baird disappeared, too. Then Hadley came running in—

Don't confuse me with Hadleys. You checked the adjacent universes.

All of them, yes. I think they're all right.

Think?

Well . . . I can't quite get back to that moment. When I disappeared. It's as if I were still there for several more seconds, so I'm excluded.

And John Baird is still there?

Not by the time I can insert myself. Just Hadley running around—

No Hadleys. No Hadleys. So, naturally, you went back to 1996.

Of course. But there is a period of several minutes there from which I'm excluded as well. When I can finally insert myself, John Baird is dead.

Ah.

In every doomline, he and Castlemaine have killed each other. John is lying there with his head blown off, Castle next to him with his heart torn out from a point-blank pistol shot, with two very distraught women and police piling in the door. And this.

The overnight bag with the stories.

I don't think anybody noticed it. With Baird dead, I could spotcheck the women's futures; neither of them mentions the bag. So perhaps the mission is accomplished.

Well, Reality is still here. So far. But the connection between Baird and this Hemingway entity is disturbing. That Baird is able to return to 1996 without your help is very disturbing. He has obviously taken on some of your characteristics, your abilities, which is why you're excluded from the last several minutes of his life.

I've never heard of that happening before.

It never has. I think John Baird is no more human than you and I.

Is?

I suspect he's still around somewhen.

29   Islands in the Stream

And the unending lightless desert of pain becomes suddenly one small bright spark and then everything is dark red and a taste, a bitter taste, Hoppe's No. 9 gun oil and the twin barrels of the fine Boss pigeon gun cold and oily on his tongue and biting hard against the roof of his mouth; the dark red is light on the other side of his eyelids, sting of pain before he bumps a tooth and opens his eyes and mouth and lowers the gun and with shaking hands unloads—no, *disloads*—both barrels and walks backward, shuffling in the slippers, slumping, stopping to stare out into the Idaho morning dark, helpless tears coursing up from the snarled white beard, walking backward down the stairs with the shotgun heavily cradled in his elbow, backing into the storeroom and replacing it in the rack, then back up the stairs and slowly put the keys there in plain sight on the kitchen windowsill, a bit of mercy from Miss Mary, then sit and stare at the cold bad coffee as it warms back to one acid sip—

A tiny part of the mind saying *wait! I am John Baird it is 1996*

and back to a spiritless shower, numb to the needle spray, and cramped constipation and a sleep of no ease; an evening with Mary and George Brown tiptoeing around the blackest of black-ass worse and worse each day, only one thing to look forward to

got to throw out an anchor

faster now, walking through the Ketchum woods like a jerky cartoon in reverse, fucking FBI and IRS behind every tree, because you sent Ezra that money, felt sorry for him because he was crazy, what a fucking joke, should have finished the Cantos and shot himself.

effect preceding cause but I can read or hear scraps of thought somehow

speeding to a blur now, driving in reverse hundreds of miles per hour back from Ketchum to Minnesota, the Mayo Clinic, holding the madness in while you talk to the shrink, promise not to hurt myself have to go home and write if I'm going to beat this, figuring what he wants to hear, then the rubber mouthpiece and smell of your own hair and flesh slightly burnt by the electrodes then deep total blackness

sharp stabs of thought sometimes stretching

hospital days blur by in reverse, cold chrome and starch white, a couple of mouthfuls of claret a day to wash down the pills that seem to make it worse and worse

what will happen to me when he's born?

When they came back from Spain was when he agreed to the Mayo Clinic, still all beat up from the plane crashes six years before in Africa, liver and spleen shot to hell, brain too, nerves, can't write or can't stop: all day on one damn sentence for the Kennedy book but a hundred thousand fast words, pure shit, for the bullfight article. Paris book okay but stuck. Great to find the trunks in the Ritz but none of the stuff Hadley lost.

Here it stops. A frozen tableau:

Afternoon light slanting in through the tall cloudy windows of the Cambon bar, where he had liberated, would liberate, the hotel in August, 1944. A good large American-style martini gulped too fast in the excitement. The two small trunks unpacked and laid out item by item. Hundreds of pages of notes that would become the Paris book. But nothing before '23, of course. *the manuscripts* The novel and the stories and the poems still gone. One moment nailed down with the juniper sting of the martini and then time crawling rolling flying backward again—

no control?

Months blurring by, Madrid Riviera Venice feeling sick and

busted up, the plane wrecks like a quick one-two punch brain and body, blurry sick even before them at the Finca Vigia, can't get a fucking thing done after the Nobel Prize, journalists day and night, the prize bad luck and bullshit anyhow but need the $35,000

damn, had to shoot Willie, cat since the boat-time before the war, but winged a burglar too, same gun, just after the Pulitzer, now that was all right

slowing down again—Havana—the Floridita—

Even Mary having a good time, and the Basque jai alai players too, though they don't know much English, most of them, interesting couple of civilians, the doctor and the Kraut lookalike, but there's something about the boy that makes it hard to take my eyes off him, looks like someone I guess, another round of Papa Dobles, that boy, what is it about him? and then the first round, with lunch, and things speeding up to a blur again

out on the Gulf a lot, enjoying the triumph of *The Old Man and the Sea*, the easy good-paying work of providing fishing footage for the movie, and then back into 1951, the worst year of his life that far, weeks of grudging conciliation, uncontrollable anger, and black-ass depression from the poisonous critical slime that followed *Across the River*, bastards gunning for him, Harold Ross dead, mother Grace dead, son Gregory a dope addict hip-deep into the dianetics horseshit, Charlie Scribner dead but first declaring undying love for that asshole Jones

most of the forties an anxious blur, Cuba Italy Cuba France Cuba China, found Mary kicked Martha out, thousand pages on the fucking *Eden* book wouldn't come together Bronze Star better than Pulitzer

Martha a chromeplated bitch in Europe but war is swell otherwise, liberating the Ritz, grenades rifles pistols and bomb runs with the RAF, China boring compared to it and the Q-ship runs off Cuba, hell, maybe the bitch was right for once, just kid stuff and booze

marrying the bitch was the end of my belle epoch, easy to
see from here, the thirties all sunshine Key West Spain West
Africa Key West, good hard writing with Pauline holding down
the store, good woman but sorry I had to

sorry I had to divorce

stopping

Walking Paris streets after midnight:

I was never going to throw back at her losing the manuscripts. Told Steffens that would be like blaming a human for the
weather, or death. These things happen. Nor say anything about
what I did the night after I found out she really had lost them.
But this one time we got to shouting and I think I hurt her. Why
the hell did she have to bring the carbons what the hell did she
think carbons were for stupid stupid stupid and she crying and
she giving me hell about Pauline Jesus any woman who could
fuck up Paris for you could fuck up a royal flush

it slows down around the manuscripts or me—

golden years the mid-twenties everything clicks Paris
Vorarlburg Paris Schruns Paris Pamplona Paris Madrid Paris Lausanne

couldn't believe she actually

most of a novel dozens of poems stories sketches—*contes*,
Kitty called them by God woman you show me your *conte* and I'll
show you mine

so drunk that night I know better than to drink that much
absinthe so drunk I was half crawling going up the stairs to the
apartment I saw weird I saw God I saw *I saw myself standing there
on the fourth landing with Hadley's goddamn bag*

I waited almost an hour, that seemed like no time or all
time, and when he, when I, when he came crashing up the stairs
he blinked twice, then I walked through me groping, shook my
head without looking back and managed to get the door un-
locked

*flying back through the dead winter French countryside, standing
in the bar car fighting hopelessness to Hadley crying so hard she can't*

get out what was wrong with Steffens standing gaping like a fish in a bowl

twisting again, painlessly inside out, I suppose through various dimensions, seeing the man's life as one complex chord of beauty and purpose and ugliness and chaos, my life on one side of the Möbius strip, consistent through its fading forty-year span, starting, *starting*, here:

the handsome young man sits on the floor of the apartment holding himself, rocking racked with sobs, one short manuscript crumpled in front of him, the room a mess with drawers pulled out their contents scattered on the floor, it's like losing an arm a leg (a foot a testicle), it's like losing your youth and along with youth

with a roar he stands up, eyes closed fists clenched, wipes his face dry and stomps over to the window

breathes deeply until he's breathing normally

strides across the room, kicking a brassiere out of his way

stands with his hand on the knob and thinks this:

life can break you but you can grow back strong at the broken places

and goes out slamming the door behind him, somewhat conscious of having been present at his own birth.

With no effort I find myself standing earlier that day in the vestibule of a train. Hadley is walking away, tired, looking for a vendor. I turn and confront two aspects of myself.

"Close your mouth, John. You'll catch flies."

They both stand paralyzed while I slide open the door and pull the overnight bag from under the seat. I walk away and the universe begins to tingle and sparkle.

I spend forever in the black void between timespaces. I am growing to enjoy it.

I appear in John Baird's apartment and set down the bag. I look at the empty chair in front of the old typewriter, the green beer bottle sweating cold next to it, and John Baird appears, looking dazed, and I have business elsewhere, elsewhen. A train to catch. I'll come back for the bag in twelve minutes or a few millenniums, after the bloodbath that gives birth to us all.

30 - 30 -

He wrote the last line and set down the pencil and read over the last page sitting on his hands for warmth. He could see his breath. Celebrate the end with a little heat.

He unwrapped the bundle of twigs and banked them around the pile of coals in the brazier. Crazy way to heat a room but it's France. He cupped both hands behind the stack and blew gently. The coals glowed red and then orange and with the third breath the twigs smoldered and a small yellow flame popped up. He held his hands over the fire, rubbing the stiffness out of his fingers, enjoying the smell of the birch as it cracked and spit.

He put a fresh sheet and carbon into the typewriter and looked at his penciled notes. Final draft? Worth a try:

```
Ernest M. Hemingway,
74 rue du Cardinal Lemoine,
Paris, France
```

```
          >> UP IN MICHIGAN >>


     Jim Gilmore came to Horton's Bay from Canada.

He bought the blacksmith shop from old man Horton
```

Shit, a typo. He flinched suddenly, as if struck, and shook his head to clear it. What a strange sensation to come out of nowhere. A sudden cold stab of grief. But larger somehow than grief for a person.

Grief for everybody, it felt like. For being human, for having to die, for having to live.

From a typo?

He went to the window and opened it in spite of the cold. He filled his lungs with the cold damp air and looked around the familiar orange-and-gray mosaic of chimney pots and tiled roofs under the dirty winter Paris sky.

He shuddered and eased the window back down and returned to the heat of the brazier. He had felt it before, exactly that huge and terrible feeling. But where?

For the life of him he couldn't remember.

Afterword

This is a work of imagination, not scholarship,[1] but there were scholars involved in its construction, and I would like to acknowledge their help here:

Thanks to Michael Reynolds for his two fine biographies of Hemingway's early life and his weird true insights into history and the nature of time.

---

[1] All of the chapter headings except the last one are titles or working titles of various Hemingway works. Please don't write and ask me to identify them. I lost the list.

Thanks to Jackson Bryer for the use of his large and quirky Hemingway collection and, wow, the beach house where part of this was written.

Thanks to Scott Donaldson and the other people at the Schruns Hemingway Conference who listened to a reading from an early version of this and made valuable comments.

Of course, any errors of fact are the result of my own ignorance or laziness, and are probably not errors in some dimension.

JOE HALDEMAN

THE LONG HABIT OF LIVING

More even than space travel, the Stileman Process had altered twenty-first century life. The most complex of medical miracles, it ensured that every ten years or so, the ailing, ageing body could be restored to youthful vigour and health.

There was a catch of course. The cost. Every ten years or so, you had to come up with £1,000,000 minimum or die.

For Dallas Barr, one of the oldest men on earth, it was that time again. It was while he was casting around for that vital next million that he came across Maria, a woman from – literally – a previous life. And made two major discoveries.

Not all Stileman 'immortals' were born – or created – the same. And someone is trying to kill them. All of them.

HODDER AND STOUGHTON PAPERBACKS

GENE WOLFE

PANDORA BY HOLLY HOLLANDER

'My name's Holly H. Hollander. The H is for Henrietta, so you can see why I don't use it.'

Born in a sprawling suburb of Chicago, Holly is an all-American girl. Kind-of-tall, long curly brown hair, a little waist she can nearly get her hands around, and a burning ambition: to write.

PANDORA is the story of an unusual box discovered at the annual antiques fair, and what happened when it was opened. It's a murder mystery, a family tale, and a love story; Holly falls for the private detective, Aladdin Blue. But it's also something else; something altogether different . . .

'Of all the SF writers active none is held in higher esteem than Gene Wolfe'

Washington Post Book World

'The double-tiered author credits on the title page perfectly expresses what the reader has in store. Candid, irrepressible Holly Hollander – and behind her that wily sleight-of-hand artist Wolfe'

Locus

HODDER AND STOUGHTON PAPERBACKS

DAVID WINGROVE

CHUNG KUO
Book Two: The Broken Wheel

There had been war – a war which the great world-spanning empire of Chung Kuo had survived. But at a cost.

The Seven – rulers of Chung Kuo – were weak. Weaker than they had ever been. Now, in the teeming lower depths of their great City, the current of change is flowing again, turning the Great Wheel, and one event – a murder, perhaps, or a palace plot – might throw the world into chaos once more.

'Why this epic continues to work so convincingly is because its social forces, and changes, within its China-orientated middle kingdom, are clarified as cleverly as Asimov's *Foundation*, while its characters give all that inexorable change a human dimension. Love, tragedy, joy and a sense of destiny being fulfilled – all human life (and death) is there. Another six volumes to go and I'm not even winded'

Tom Hutchinson in The Times

'Extraordinary'

Brian Aldiss

HODDER AND STOUGHTON PAPERBACKS

C. J. CHERRYH

RIMRUNNERS

Elizabeth Yeager: spacer, machinist, temp. Unemployed now. Registering for ship work on a bypassed, dying star base where the big ships no longer call.

Until the *Loki* docks. A spook: a mercenary warship free-lancing as a space bounty hunter with a captain who's not too worried about proper papers or charges pending when he hires.

Bet Yeager: an outsider in a crew of brutalised misfits operating on the edge of legality and the far rim of inter-stellar civilisation . . .

'One of the finest writers SF has to offer'

SF Chronicle

'Close-quarters tension, with never a dull moment and rarely a safe one . . . This is a book you *live* in the reading'

Locus

HODDER AND STOUGHTON PAPERBACKS

JOHN CRAMER

TWISTOR

Original, elegant and profound, the discovery of the Twistor effect held out infinite promise. For the first time, it brought alternate universes within reach of human exploration.

To physicist David Harrison, the prospect was of new, unspoilt Edens.

To the Megalith Corporation the prospect was of the ultimate in exploitable resources and power.

'True hard science fiction – deftly done, with plenty of fine surprises'

Gregory Benford

'The most exciting novel about the cutting edge of physics since *Timescape* ... Takes you into the lab and through the world of far-out theory, all in a swooping story of adventure'

David Brin

'*Twistor* marks the arrival of a major new science-fiction talent'

Gene Wolfe

HODDER AND STOUGHTON PAPERBACKS